THE LOOP BREAKER

A Beacon and the Darkness

RUSS THOMPSON

Winterwolf Press

Library of Congress Control Number: 2020939588

ISBN: 978-1-947782-06-8

First Edition

This is a work of fiction. Names, characters, places, and incidents are either products of the author's imagination or are used fictitiously. Any resemblance to actual persons, living or dead, businesses, jobs, companies, events, or locations is entirely coincidental and/or fictional. The author and publisher assume no responsibility for any errors, false information, or omissions. No liability is assumed for damages that may result from the reading or use of information contained within. The views of this publication do not necessarily reflect the views of Winterwolf Press.

Books may be purchased by contacting the publisher and author at:

www.WinterwolfPress.com

Info@WinterwolfPress.com

Social Media @WinterwolfPress

Edited by Laura Jones

Cover art by José Suárez

Interior design and formatting by Laura C. Cantu

Cover design © 2020 Winterwolf Press

CHAPTER 1
YOU DON'T NEED TO HOLD ON

B rushing back long, dyed-black hair from her shoulders, Lee
Ann blinked her large doleful eyes and took a deep breath.
She looked away from the full-length mirror in her bedroom,
began to remove the large collection of bracelets she always wore and
set them on her dresser. She recently had her bangs cut shorter than
their usual length, leaving the rest of it long and was still deciding if
she liked it or not. She looked back toward the mirror, shook her hair
out and played with her bangs. At that moment, she decided she did
like her new look.

Just after she turned fifteen a little over a year ago, her height
seemed to double, her shoulders broadened, and her legs grew longer.
Much to the consternation of both sets of her parents, she got her
nose pierced six months ago. She and her best friend, Hanna, had met
up with Johnny Garland, a senior at their high school who worked at a
tattoo parlor. Johnny snuck the job in on one of his boss' days off. Lee
Ann sat twisting the ring on her nostril as she thought about how
lucky she had been when they only grounded her for a week. Punish-
ment was not on her radar; she had hardly ever been in trouble.

That was a happier time, however; a time before she became
unable to hide the expression of loss behind her prominent brows and

wide, brown eyes. Lately, Lee Ann spent most of the day staring at the ground or at the space between her knees. Her full lips, often closed in silence, gave people the mistaken impression that she was pouting.

She took a deep breath and gazed back at her image. She half-expected the door to her bedroom to open at any moment and for her mother, Kim, to walk through. Before Kim's passing, her unexpected appearance would have been an intrusion, but if it were to happen now, it would be the most welcome sight. Lee Ann couldn't remember the last time she'd smiled; she was certain it was before her mother's passing.

For a moment, Lee Ann stared at the door, pretending she could will her mother to appear. she imagined smelling the rose-scented Crabtree and Evelyn perfume her mother liked to wear, and pictured her warm, hazel eyes, which always seemed widened with concern and love. She saw her mother's brownish-blonde hair pulled up in a pony-tail, as it so often was.

The memory of her mother's figure in her doorway was nearly as vivid as another memory that kept replaying in her mind. On the third day following her mother's death, when everyone but Lee Ann's grand-mother and stepfather, Daniel, had left, Lee Ann went to sit on the swing on the front porch where she and her mother would have occa-sional heart-to-hearts. Despite the usual invasion of privacy sixteen-year-olds generally feel when their parents try to pry into their lives, Lee Ann now longed for probing questions, for that knowing glint in her mother's eyes. That day, as she sat on the porch swing, she allowed herself to be carried back to the night, just seven months ago, after she found out her boyfriend was seeing someone else at school, and recalled her mother's comforting words.

"He was never right for you, dear. I could tell when he first walked in that he had that wolf-in-sheep's-clothing look. Also, he wasn't into anything you were into. He was only interested in football, and he wasn't even very good at it. It would have never worked," Kim had said, inspiring a laugh from Lee Ann. Kim echoed her daughter's laughter and kissed her head. Although she had already known what her mother told her to be true, hearing the words offered her comfort and solace.

For just a moment, as she remembered that conversation, Lee Ann had felt the comfort and security that she felt that night, just months ago, when she sat on the same swing. Sitting there again in the days following her mother's death, the words Kim had shared that night echoed through Lee Ann's head, as if ushered through the nearby trees on the breeze. The sound seemed to originate from an area of space just beside Lee Ann.

"You don't need to hold on." Lee Ann could hear her mother's words, yet was unable to tell if the words formed from her own memory, like a lucid dream in a waking state, or if the voice she heard was actually her mother speaking in the here and now. Lee Ann had felt the essence of her mother beside her and caught a glimpse, however fleeting, of her mother's tender smile; she even saw the subtle creases of her dimples. Lee Ann scooted toward where her mother had sat, and as she closed her eyes, she could feel the warmth of her touch. When she opened her eyes, Lee Ann was floating in a space that was alien to her, surrounded by darkness. It was like being suspended in a night sky, twinkling with the spectral light of myriad stars. It was not a fearful place, but a place of mystery. The porch swing was gone; it was just she and her mother hovering there suspended in space. No explanation was given other than the grin and thoughtful gaze her mother always shared with her, one that seemed to communicate the rightness of things and their necessity. Then, the setting and the feeling of peace faded quickly as the slight wind, the one that carried her mother's voice, retreated into the distance.

Tears had followed then and would flow for days.

Kim's passing was not sudden, but long and drawn out. The cancer was far too prevalent when it was diagnosed, spreading from Kim's lungs into muscle and bone tissue. Daniel had urged Lee Ann to stay away from the hospital the last few days, but he could not pull her from her mother's bedside. Lee Ann had not let go of her mother's hand and continued to grip it tightly even after her mother gave her that knowing, 'it's going to be alright,' look of wisdom that had comforted Lee Ann through so many hardships.

Firmly rooting herself back in the present, she found herself back in her room again. She took a deep breath and gazed upon the pictures of her and her mother that she had arranged in chronological order along the bottom of the small antique mirror on her dresser.

There was the picture of Lee Ann's first birthday with a Big Bird cake placed in front of her. Kim had longer hair and youthful clothes, smiling beside the beaming baby. The last picture in the chronology showed Lee Ann and her mother in their kitchen just weeks before Kim's diagnosis. Both of them still had the same smiles, fifteen years later; smiles that seemed ignorant and selfish now in the wake of her mother's suffering. Lee Ann looked up from the pictures at her own sallow face in the mirror. There were dark circles and puffy, red cheeks making her appear much older than she was. Her neck and shoulders seemed to hang loosely under her black t-shirt, belying the lack of sustenance she had provided herself over the last couple of weeks in the depths of her mourning. The bright tint in her large, usually hopeful eyes seemed to have lost some of their luster.

Lee Ann let out a long, deep sigh just as the sound of a vehicle on the gravel driveway outside of their suburban home caught her attention. She grabbed her tan satchel, which was covered with buttons, and jumped to look out the window to make sure it wasn't her mother's red Honda pulling away. Kim would do that, fake leaving, in an attempt to rush Lee Ann so she wouldn't be late for school.

Punctuality was never Lee Ann's strong suit, but ever since her mother's passing, she'd been on time for school. All of the faults that her mother had pointed out in her subtle, supportive way, Lee Ann had sought to remedy. There were no more dishes piled in the corner of her room, and she dare not open her laptop or answer any of Hanna's texts until all of her homework was done.

The mirage of the red Honda turned into an aged blue Ford truck that rattled in the driveway as if it might explode into a pile of nuts and bolts at any moment. It was Lee Ann's father, Charles, who'd just arrived to take her away. She cast her eyes to the ceiling and flared her nostrils.

For three weeks now, Charles had been ready to take Lee Ann home with him once and for all. However, Lee Ann insisted she be allowed to stay with Daniel at least until fall break. After some initial resistance, Charles relented, seeing the pained look in his daughter's eyes. He recognized the need she had for closure in the home she had shared with her mother.

The day had finally come when Lee Ann would leave what she knew behind. After all, although Daniel longed to maintain a relationship with her, he would not have been able to gain custody of his stepdaughter. Daniel and Lee Ann had always maintained a friendly yet detached rapport that had grown into something much more tender over the last few weeks. He'd gone out of his way to make Lee Ann's favorite meals and allowed her to do much of what she wanted to. They had even embraced a time or two when the living memory of Kim was too much for them in the silence of the house. Lee Ann was the last surviving remnant of the woman he loved so dearly.

In that moment, Lee Ann tried to push back against the resentment that she felt toward her father as he got out of his beat-up pickup truck. The emotion took her back to a memory from when she was nine. The memory took place in the driveway of their old house where they lived in Laverne; her parents had shouted at one another before her father left them for the last time.

"Maybe she will tolerate your drinking more than I could!" Kim had shouted as the truck spun out in the driveway, throwing pieces of gravel against the metal railing of the porch.

Following the divorce proceedings, shortly after that fateful day, Lee Ann began spending every other weekend at her father's house, about an hour and a half away. Now that she was sixteen, she could have chosen not to visit him any longer had her mother not lost her battle with cancer. In her mother's absence, her father could claim full custody and take her away from all that she knew.

Regaining her strength, Lee Ann gathered the pictures of her mother one-by-one and carefully placed them in one of her suitcases. It was the last thing she had to pack. She slung her satchel over her shoulder, put on her oversized army-green jacket, and picked up her two suitcases. She paused briefly to ponder the now empty mirror, devoid of the pictures that acted as a storyboard of the life Lee Ann knew was over.

You still there, L? her friend Hanna texted her a second later.

Not much longer. Headed out now. Don't worry, I'll be back soon.

I know you will. Try not to let the boredom get to you. I'll text you every night.

I know.

Don't let those redneck boys take you on a hunt or to one of their bonfires.

Don't worry, Hanna.

Love you.

Love you more.

In the foyer, Daniel, having just gotten home from work, stood tall with his usual suit on. He looked something like a funeral director. His face was long and grim with a generous amount of black stubble. His thinning, dark hair was slicked slightly back, and the expression on his face was a mixture of resignation and compassion. Without a word, as she reached the bottom of the stairs, Daniel and Lee Ann exchanged a final glance. Lee Ann had to look down at her baggage to avoid the return of her tears.

"Lee, I want you to know that you will always have a home here. Whenever you want to come back and visit, I will be glad to have you," Daniel said, knowing his words were inadequate for the gravity of the situation.

"I know," Lee Ann replied. Dropping her bags, she suddenly threw her arms around him. He closed his eyes and hugged her back, feeling the warm tears forming in the corners of his eyes.

"Come on, don't keep your father waiting," he said, glancing for a second into Lee Ann's watery eyes. He looked away quickly for fear of being consumed with despair.

Outside, Charles approached the door in an unhurried gait. He wore a brown coat with a blue hoodie protruding underneath. Unlike Daniel's sleek, put together look, Charles looked like a rugged outdoorsman. His face was stained with red stubble and his brown hair seemed overly curly and wild for a man in his mid-forties.

"You ready, Punkin?" he said with his usual drawl as he came over to Lee Ann's side and picked up her suitcases.

Daniel stood in the doorway watching them, trying to distance himself from the situation.

"I'm too old to be called Punkin, Dad," Lee Ann replied.

"Got it." He cast his eyes over to Daniel and gave him a half-smile.

After putting Lee Ann's bags in the backseat, he walked over to Daniel with his hands in his pockets.

"Daniel, I want you to know how much I appreciate everything you've done for my daughter. I won't forget it," Charles said, thrusting his hand out for a shake. Lee Ann watched from outside the passenger's side of the truck.

Daniel nodded his head, shook Charles' hand and smiled slightly. "She will always be welcome here," he replied.

"Well, I sure am thankful for that," he answered, making direct eye contact as he continued to shake Daniel's hand firmly.

"You can thank me by allowing her to come to visit," Daniel said, casting his eyes over at Lee Ann who smiled back.

"Of course, after she settles in," Charles said.

"Of course," Daniel echoed.

Charles gave him another half-smile and walked around to the driver's side of his truck. Lee Ann hesitated for a moment, taking in the sight of her home one last time. Its ordinary white suburban columns and shutters now seemed more extraordinary and individual than they once had. She let her eyes land on Daniel one last time and got in the musty-smelling truck.

"You alright?" Charles asked her.

"Yes," she answered simply, not wanting to discuss the matter further. She turned her head toward the window to hide the tears that threatened to flood her cheeks.

"Lee Ann, I know this is hard for you, but it's for the best. I'm your father and you need to come live with me now. It's the way things oughta be," he said.

She didn't answer as she watched the pine trees that lined the drive whizz by. Over the last few years, Lee Ann's relationship with him had been strained. Charles had gone out of his way to please his daughter and try to chip away the resentment she felt over his leaving. He'd tried to explain to her that he had to go away to get 'better' and deal with his drinking problem, but it always seemed to fall flat. It was as if he were explaining himself to an empty cave that would do nothing but echo his words back at him. Even though Lee Ann felt his words as hollow, she still loved and needed him. She just didn't want it to show, and therefore maintained a hard exterior and a stiff upper lip like she always did when she was in avoidance mode.

"You're going to like the new place. I know how much you hated our house in town. I promise you this is a vast improvement. I got the whole property for a song; it was a foreclosure. Now, I have a building that I can convert into a new mechanics shop and fifteen acres of woods with a creek," Charles revealed as the excitement in his voice increased. Lee Ann perked up a bit at this news and looked over at him.

Despite being a city girl, she loved to go hiking in the woods. When she wasn't sketching something in her journal or on her computer, she was hiking at Radnor Lake or on the Natchez Trace outside Nashville. Her idea of a pleasant Saturday afternoon was taking her sketchbook to a lonely hillside and re-creating the landscape in pencil.

Often, Hanna would come along and talk the whole time, as she usually did. Kim had referred to her as the Mouth of the South; however, Lee Ann didn't mind, she enjoyed her friend's talkative nature. It was as if Hanna's boisterous persona balanced out her subtle quietness. At school, Hanna would be the one boys always talked to first because she was not shy about starting a conversation. With her short bob and perky mannerisms, she was very much her best friend's opposite. Lee Ann would often just listen, keeping her eyes downcast as the boys' eyes washed over her tall, thin figure, which she kept hidden in baggy clothes.

"It has a creek?" she asked, hopefully.

"Yes, it's pretty shallow, but there are a few pools deep enough to swim and even some fishing spots. Not that you're big on fishing, really," he said.

Lee Ann looked back out the window at the pastoral scenery. The crowded suburbs and traffic of Nashville began to give way to steep hills and thick forest. The trees draped the middle Tennessee land-scape—thousands of gnarled, wooden hands grasping for the autumn sky, freckled with the red, yellow, and orange onslaught of fall. Lee Ann liked to imagine what scenes and secrets lay hidden by the thick woods. For a moment, her thoughts turned from the despair of leaving her home and were lost in the landscape she witnessed.

"What're you thinking over there?" Charles asked. Any prolonged silence made him feel uncomfortable, especially when he was with his daughter. He wanted to distract her from any resentful feelings she may be harboring toward him.

"Oh nothing," she offered, honestly.

"You can tell me, you know. You always can," he put his hand on her shoulder.

"I know, Dad," she said, half-heartedly, giving him a short, sideways glance.

"We're going to have some good times you and me, you'll see," he offered in an attempt to cheer her up.

Lee Ann looked back out the window, thinking that her father was dangerously close to overplaying his hand; whenever he tried too hard to gain her approval and affection, he never seemed to get through to her. The extra effort made the hour and a half drive seem to drag on forever. To escape her discomfort, she put on her headphones to listen to the new album by St. Vincent. The electronic soundscape paired with Annie Clark's emotional vocals overwhelmed Lee Ann.

"How could anybody have you and lose you and not lose their minds, too?" she sang, and although the words were about a lost love affair, they reminded Lee Ann of her mother again. She quickly switched to a silly song by Devo, which eased her mood.

Soon the highway gave way to a winding two-lane road through a thick forest. Every now and again, a house or run-down barn came into view, but the further they drove, the less there was evidence of any inhabitants. It was like entering a scene from another century. Just when Lee Ann thought they couldn't possibly probe any deeper into the woodlands, a gravel drive with a green gate appeared to their left.

"This is it," Charles said as he put the truck into park, hopping out to unlock the gate.

"How far are the nearest neighbors?" Lee Ann asked, wondering aloud more than actually asking a question.

"About two miles or so. It's what I've always wanted, Punkin—

complete seclusion even though it's actually only a short walk to town," he said with a mischievous grin.

His wife, Shirley, was less happy with the arrangement, although she acquiesced when she saw the spacious kitchen in the old country house. Shirley also was not thrilled with the prospect of her step-daughter coming to live with them permanently. Having little use for children and having none of her own, she had always had a hard time relating to Lee Ann. Lee Ann kept her distance, feeling no need for motherly attention from this aloof woman her father married.

The driveway wound back nearly half a mile through the woods past an old, wooden barn and storage building before connecting with a circular gravel drive in front of what looked to be a centuries-old, white farmhouse. There was a long side porch that attached to a circular, tower-like structure with multiple windows that seemed to glare outward. Its white façade was chipped, peeling and in bad need of a new coat of paint. Just beyond and to the left of the house was a garden, overgrown with dying vines stymied by the oncoming winter chill.

"Well, here we are," Charles said, pausing to gaze at his new acquisition through the windshield of the truck. Lee Ann gazed at it herself, feeling a mixture of emotions.

"You have to try and see what it could be, not what it is," Charles said, sensing his daughter's dissatisfaction.

"I know," she said, opening the door of the truck to escape the awkward silence that followed.

CHAPTER 2
A WHISPER ON THE WIND

In a sense, Lee Ann returned to her roots when she moved in with her father—she and her family were from Pearson County, where the country house sat. The hills, clothed in thick oaks and hickories with networks of creeks, were woven into her DNA, even if she didn't care to admit it.

She walked up the rotting stairs onto the front porch of the old farmhouse and thought back to her childhood, when her mother and father lived in a modest home in the heart of this same tiny town: Laverne. So tiny, the latest census indicated it still hadn't reached the one thousand mark. In fact, the entire county had little more than a few thousand inhabitants scattered in tiny towns or living in carved out patches from the forest, in between the tree-clad hills.

With each step, she felt as if she were retreating into a past that she'd already escaped from—like the time her mother married Daniel and moved them to the Nashville suburbs when she was nine. Lee Ann hadn't felt entirely at home in this setting either. After Lee Ann reached her teenage years, the well-dressed neighbors would give her occasional looks of disdain, which she attributed to her choice of dress —usually a black t-shirt and maybe a flannel if the weather was cooler.

She tended toward more earthy, drab colors and loved to wear leggings with short skirts and her converse sneakers or combat boots.

You people don't know me and I sure don't want to know you, she would think to herself as she walked through what she felt was a cookie cutter neighborhood with large, but overly-similar houses. When they first moved to Nashville, she was excited about her new environment. However, as she grew older, she began to become more conscious of the differences between her and the neighbors. Here in Laverne she felt cast into yet another setting where she didn't quite fit.

She stopped at the door of her new home, wondering how old the metal screen door was with its torn interlacing leaf pattern.

"Go on in, it ain't locked," Charles laughed with his usual grin that Lee Ann would refer to as 'shit-eating' when she described it to Hanna. Lee Ann walked through a small foyer and through a large room with high ceilings and peeling, off-white paint on the walls. The floors were littered with boxes. She sighed and reminded herself that her father had only recently moved there.

"Remember: try to picture what it's going to be," Charles interjected, sensing Lee Ann's hesitation.

A mahogany staircase wound up to the upper floor, hinting at the house's former elegance. She decided to venture upstairs and explore. When she reached the top of the stairs, she could hear her father walking slowly behind her, coming to gauge her response to her new home.

"That's your room off to the left. I chose that one for you because it has the best view of the woods behind the house," he shared. Lee Ann turned toward him for a second and gave him a small smile. She appreciated her father's efforts to make her feel more at home, although this was anything but home for her at this stage.

Lee Ann stepped into the room and threw her satchel on the bed, which made all the attached buttons rattle. She was pleased to see that the paint wasn't peeling in the room as it was downstairs and that the room was well lit, allowing plentiful sunshine in from two large windows. She made her way to the window and looked out at the wilderness beyond the overgrown lawn behind the house. To the left, she caught a glimpse of the weed-choked garden and a statue of a cherub pouring water into a stone fountain with a small bucket just beyond a small storage shed. Her eyes shifted back to the woods, which seemed solemn and secretive beneath the thin light that snuck through an ashen sky, laced with clouds. Lee Ann felt curiosity accompanied by a feeling of dread that she could not put her finger on. It was as if there were a secret that she wanted to unlock, but also a wariness that tugged at her.

Charles peered into the room from just outside the doorway,

"I'm going to go downstairs and fix us some lunch. I'll let you settle in and call you down when it's ready," he said with a smile. Lee Ann turned from the window and smiled at him.

"Where's Shirley?" she asked suddenly.

"Oh, she's in town. She took a job manning the dentist's office. Not really her thing, but it will help pay the mortgage on this place," he explained before turning to go back down the steps.

Lee Ann sat on the bed facing the window. In the silence of this new room, she felt totally and utterly alone, abandoned by her former life and the love of her mother. Without warning, tears began to spill. She buried her head in her hands and let long sobs take her over, leaving her gasping in her despair. Then, as quickly as they had begun, the tears halted and she managed to catch her breath. For a moment, in that place, her mourning seemed almost absurd and useless; there seemed to be no one that cared and nothing to be gained from sorrow. It drained from her like the water slowing dripping from the pitcher held by the cherub statue outside her window.

When she had first arrived, her father had left a box of her things on the floor. She opened it to unpack its contents. She eagerly pulled out a black and white cat clock that her mother gave her, which she hung on a nail that had been left on the wall beside the bed. For a few minutes, she lay on the bed and looked up at it; it made her smile to have a piece of her old life here with her, reminding her that there were plenty of happy memories to celebrate.

Despite the futility of her tears, Lee Ann felt a bit better as she dried her face with a tissue from the bedside table, threw her bag over her shoulder and turned to go back down the stairs.

Once she reached the kitchen, she listened to the sounds of her father spreading mayonnaise on the bread. Lee Ann had always been hypersensitive to sounds that others were scarcely aware of. In fact, it was often a source of distraction when she was trying to concentrate on something such as her homework.

She tried to walk silently by the door toward the exit, but Charles heard her.

"Where you off to, Punkin?"

"Dad . . ."

"Oh, sorry. Where you off to, dear?"

"Thought I'd go exploring down by the creek," she said, trying to turn her face away from him so that he wouldn't notice the remnants of her tears.

"You alright?"

"I'll be fine," she responded, turning the knob on the back door.

"Lee Ann," he said in an imploring tone.

"Yes?" she asked, turning back toward him.

"Give it some time. I know it's a cliché but time heals all wounds and all that."

"Got it, Dad," she answered with another half smile. As she exited the back door, she shook her head and laughed slightly at her father's attempts to soothe her. Ever since she turned thirteen, it seemed that Charles was doing his best to try and break through the cool, cynical façade of his daughter. Although he wanted desperately to be closer to her and know who she was, the truth was, he knew very little.

Her bitterness toward him had resulted in many short and stilted conversations. Sometimes, Lee Ann would rebuke herself, wondering if she was being too cruel toward him. Then, she would remember that summer when she was nine and her mother ran out into the front yard screaming at him, her face red and streaked with tears.

"Who the hell is she, Charles?" Lee Ann recalled standing in the doorway, not recognizing the usually temperate features of her mother whose kind, hazel eyes had turned bright red.

"Nobody," he'd answered in a drunken slur. "It didn't mean anything . . ."

Lee Ann shook her head to banish the memory and opened the creaky back door. The soft wind in the branches of the trees and the distant calls of unseen birds soothed her mind. Leaves of the dying days of autumn crunched beneath her feet as she ignored the tangled garden to her left and made her way to the edge of the woods. To the south, the trees were mature and ancient, seemingly untouched by the logger's saw. The remains of an old barbed wire fence punctuated the landscape. To the north of the fencing, the trees were younger and skinnier, and Lee Ann wondered if there had once been a field here. Just inside the older trees, Lee Ann could hear the calming flow of gentle waters leaping over stones and splashing in unseen places.

The soothing sounds inspired a rare grin to creep across Lee Ann's face, showing an inner beauty that she'd kept hidden behind her despair. Upon reaching the creek, Lee Ann immediately rolled up the pant legs of her cargo pants, took off her checkerboard Vans and began to wade. Here the creek was shallow, but further downstream she could see where deeper pools formed and saw the splashing of small fish. The water in the gravel-lined stream was ice-cold and crystal clear. Beneath Lee Ann's feet, minnows with bright iridescent red stripes scattered. Occasionally, a curious brown and green darter swam around her toes. Lee Ann smiled, gazing down at the abundant life around her.

Back in the kitchen, Charles finished making the sandwiches. He went out the back door in search of Lee Ann. He was just about to call her name when he spied her skipping a stone across the surface of the water. The sight made him smile and called to mind a memory; of Lee Ann skipping stones on a canoe trip they had taken when she was eight. It gave him hope that she could still find pleasure in the simple things and move beyond the pain of her recent loss. He made his way to the edge of the woods and called out to her.

"Sandwich?" he asked. Lee Ann looked up suddenly, changing her expression as if she didn't want her father to see her moment of revelry.

"Sure," she answered in a deadpan tone.

"Pretty back here, ain't it?" he enthused.

"How far back does our property go?" she inquired. Hearing her call it 'our' property caused a slight leap in Charles' heart.

"About a half mile in that direction and a quarter of a mile on the north side of the creek," he answered. Just as his statement was uttered, a high-pitched, mournful wind rustled the leaves of an ancient oak just a few yards south of where Lee Ann stood. She looked up at the moving limbs, feeling a peculiar sensation. The breeze moved on and the limbs of the wooden sentinel became motionless again. Lee Ann pushed the feeling from her mind, dismissing it as just the mutterings of the wind and waded back to the rocks on the edge of the brook.

Charles sat down on a cracked stone bench that lay between the garden and the edge of the forest. Lee Ann came out of the woods and sat down beside him. He handed her a turkey sandwich and tore into his own. She began to eat hers in silence, still staring at the area where the breeze had moved the trees.

"What's beyond our property, over toward the south?" she asked.

"Lots more woods. A couple thousand or so acres from what I hear, most of it is a wildlife refuge," he said.

"Oh," Lee Ann said, pleased to hear this.

"I'm glad you're taking to this place. Truth is, I've been dreading this day," he confessed.

She looked at him in surprise.

"Not that I was dreadin' having you come to live with us—quite the contrary. It's just that, well, I was afraid that you'd resent me for bringin' you back to Laverne. For takin' you away from your home back in Franklin."

Lee Ann was unsure of what to say. A part of her wanted to reach over and hug him and tell him he didn't need to feel that way, but when she looked into his eyes, she thought about all his flaws that she couldn't forgive. Dark circles surrounded his drowsy, brown eyes, a byproduct of too many drinking binges. His hands were rough and calloused from working on so many car engines and transmissions. However, in his doubtful grin, she saw a fragile man reaching out to her with love and compassion. She looked away and opted for the middle ground.

"Truth is it wasn't much of a life you took me from. I didn't fit in there any more than I am likely to fit in here. All I had was Hanna and an ex-boyfriend who wouldn't leave me alone in the hallway," she revealed. Charles smiled and laughed gently at this.

"Fittin' in is overrated. Besides, give it time and you'll find your crowd even 'round here," he reassured her.

"So, who will have me?" she asked. Then to lighten the mood she added, "Will it be the hunters or the farmers?" Charles' smile vanished. He couldn't see the humor in her words. His daughter's snobbery with regard to the people of the country rubbed him the wrong way.

"Not everyone here is a hunter or a farmer," he corrected her.

"Just ninety-nine percent of them," she said looking back toward the creek again.

"Maybe if you just think of people as people you could find someone you connect with," he suggested. Lee Ann got up and began to roll her pant legs back down again.

"Will the others do the same when they meet me?" she asked in a challenging way.

"If you give them a chance," Charles said with a slightly agitated tone. With that, he turned around quickly to go back in the house. Lee Ann's eyes followed him; she felt bad for making him upset.

"Dad, wait. I'm sorry. I was being too much of a city snob," she explained.

Charles turned around and gave her a slight smile.

"All I'm askin' for you to do is try and keep an open mind about your new home," he responded.

"Will do, dad," she said, smiling back at him before he continued to make his way toward the house.

Lee Ann took out her sketchbook from her satchel and began to draw the wooded landscape in front of her.

From the kitchen window, Charles watched his daughter as he washed his plate. Shirley abruptly opened the door and walked in, hanging her purse on a hook by the door. She flipped a long, dark strand of her hair out of her brown eyes and checked her image in the mirror hanging to the left of the front door. A face with high cheekbones, bold, red lipstick, and eyes surrounded by heavy eyeliner stared back. Shirley always made sure that she was dressed to impress, whether it was a day at the office or a trip to the corner store, although in Charles' opinion it was always a bit too much of a production.

"Hey, honey, how was work?" Charles asked sheepishly.

"Fine, as usual. Is she here yet?"

"Out back."

Shirley cast her eyes toward the back of the house and through the windows of the kitchen.

"Gina needed help with the scheduling, so I branched out from my usual phone duty. Also, Dale was out today so people didn't have to tiptoe around as much . . ."

The door opened and closed, halting Shirley's account of the goings on at the dentist's office.

"Hello," Lee Ann greeted, haltingly.

"Hi there. Enjoying the view out back? Nice isn't it?"

"Yes," Lee Ann answered with a nervous smile.

"Well, I'm pooped. I'm going to go soak in a hot bath for a little while," Shirley stated quickly in an attempt to avoid delving into further conversation with her stepdaughter.

"Nice talk," Lee Ann said after Shirley was up the stairs and out of range.

"Now Lee, she's had a long day," Charles broke in.

"So what's the excuse for all of the other conversations between us that go nowhere?"

Charles placed both hands on the counter and shook his head. For years, he'd been searching through his mind to figure out a way to bridge the awkward exchanges Lee Ann and Shirley always had, but he had failed to get further than suggesting to Shirley that she ask Lee Ann more questions about her own life and try to find some common ground. To which, Shirley had recently responded: "What if there isn't any? I see the look in her eyes whenever I walk in the room. It's a 'you're not my mother, why are you here?' look."

"Yes, but you're the adult. You have to show her that you care about her," Charles had said.

"You're one to talk about being an adult. How about that mechanic shop? How far away are you from being ready to open it, hun?" she responded as she walked into the next room. From that moment on, Charles had left it alone hoping that it would resolve itself over time, but since the advent of Lee Ann's teens, they had only seemed to grow more distant.

Just as Lee Ann moved toward the cabinets to get a glass, Hanna texted her.

L, what's up?

Stepmother's ignoring me as usual. You?

Ugh, what's her deal?

Heck if I know.

"Dad, I'm going up to my room for a bit," she said.

"Ok. Hey, maybe in a bit you can come down and help Shirley with dinner," he suggested.

"Maybe, uh, sure," Lee Ann said before fleeing for the stairs.

Steve will not stop asking how you are, Hanna texted.

Tell him I'm dead inside as usual.

Haha! No, really he misses you so much.

Already? Lol, he needs to give it up.

Think you'll ever forgive him?

Would you?

I don't know. I know he messed up by kissing Rebecca, but he seemed so

sincere the last time he apologized.

Well, why don't you date him?

Please!

If it's okay with you, I'd rather change the subject.

Sure. So when do I get to come and visit?

You want to come here?

You're right, I guess I can wait until you come back.

Lee Ann tossed her phone on the bed and sat looking out the window. The packed suitcases were still sitting to the right of the bed. She resisted unpacking them, hoping she might awaken from a dream and be back in her old room. Instead, the sunlight began to fade behind the trees, leaving the overgrown garden draped with long shadows. As the wind bent the tops of the trees, Lee Ann wondered if it was sighing the peculiar way it had earlier.

It's nothing, she reassured herself, propping her arms behind her head.

She thought about how people were helpless to control the circum-stances that befell them; they either swayed with the breeze or broke into pitiless sticks upon the ground to be forgotten.

CHAPTER 3
WORLDS STRANGE AND NEW

The week of fall break passed by quickly. Lee Ann spent the better part of it settling into her new home, but toward the end of the break, she returned to Franklin to visit Daniel and Hanna. Sadly, what she had looked forward to with excitement turned out to be a much different experience. The time spent at the old house only stoked the memory of the loss of her mother, which seemed to hover over everything; this made it a much heavier experience than she had intended. Lee Ann, overburdened by the memories that continuously flooded into her thoughts, would eventually cut her visit short a day.

One of her last happy memories before Kim's diagnosis was the makeover she had allowed her mother to give her. Lee Ann was reminded of it when she saw a picture on the mantle of her mother wearing the same blue dress that she'd worn that very same day.

"You don't like the dress do you?" Kim asked, referring to a floral print dress she'd bought her after a trip to the mall.

"Mom, you know what I like," Lee Ann responded.

"I know you and I know that's your way of saying you don't like it. Why? Because it isn't black or edgy enough?"

"Not everything I wear is black."

"That's like Dracula saying he doesn't always wear a cape," Daniel chimed in.

"You're not helping," Lee Ann scowled.

"Just try it on. Then, I promise I'll take it back if you hate the way it looks."

"Alright, alright," Lee Ann acquiesced, rolling her eyes.

A few minutes later, Lee Ann came out of the bathroom with the dress on. She hadn't given up her favorite combat boots or changed her hair, which was still pulled back in the usual manner. She was glad her long bangs hung down in her eyes because it helped to hide her feelings. The dress complimented her long legs and highlighted her figure in a way that her regular clothes did not and left Lee Ann feeling self-conscious.

"Wow, dear! Lose the boots, and pull that hair tie out for a change!" her mother insisted. "Here, try these," her mother said, producing a pair of short-heeled shoes from behind her back.

"What? Ugh, okay," She pulled out the hair tie and kicked off her boots. Her hair fell to her shoulders as she slipped on the shoes.

"WOW!" Kim said, turning Lee Ann toward the mirror. Daniel stood behind them watching.

"Doesn't she look beautiful, Daniel?" Kim asked.

"Indeed!" he agreed. Lee Ann smirked at the image in the mirror but did not respond.

"Can I take it off now?" she asked.

"Ugh, alright," Kim huffed, throwing her hands up. "I guess I'll take it back tomorrow."

Lee Ann began to walk away but then turned toward her mother.

"No, I'll keep it. I can wear it on Easter or something," she said. Kim's face lit up in such a way that it emblazoned the memory in Lee Ann's brain; it was the last time her mother would display anything other than a slight grin following her diagnosis.

Lee Ann came back to the present as Hanna's voice broke the spell she was under. "Where are you right now?" Hanna asked, waving a hand in front of Lee Ann's face sitting across from her on the bed.

"Sorry, this is why I need to leave early. I'm overwhelmed by memories." Unable to hold back any longer, she put her head in her hands letting an emotional dam burst.

"L, it's okay," Hanna said quickly throwing her arms around her. Lee Ann welcomed the embrace, despite the fact that she was not very touchy-feely. "Your mother was amazing; I'm sure that the last thing she would want is to see you suffer like this." Hanna pulled away slightly to make eye contact with her.

"Thanks, Hanna. I know you're right, but it's just so hard."

"Give it time. I'm always here when you need to chat."

Her father's red truck pulled up to take her back to the country, and she wiped a tear from the corner of her eye, thinking again of how happy her mother was the day before her diagnosis and how much she missed those moments.

"Dad's here, I gotta go," Lee Ann declared as she threw her arms around her best friend.

"Love you, L," Hanna said, trying to be strong and hide her emotions.

"Love you more," Lee Ann responded. She sighed, grabbed her bag and headed toward the door.

Daniel was waiting by the door, wearing a cheerful grin.

"I can't tell you how much having you back has brightened up this house, even if it's only for a short time. You will come back soon, won't you?" Daniel implored.

"Of course," she replied insistently before giving him a long hug.

"Take care, Lee Ann," he told her, his voice shaky.

"You too," she quickly replied and turned to leave for fear that she might burst into tears.

"You alright?" Charles asked when Lee Ann got in the car.

"I'm good," Lee Ann said, not wanting to dredge up the memory again.

On the morning of Lee Ann's first day at Pearson County High, she woke up early. She walked to the closet and looked at her wardrobe, thinking about first impressions. In the end, she picked out the floral-print dress her mother bought her but wore her combat boots with it.

As usual, she did not apply any makeup. On numerous occasions she had been told that she didn't need to wear makeup since she'd inherited her mother's dark eyebrows and large, round eyes, to which she'd responded, "Who needs makeup?"

Charles pulled right up to the front door of the school.

"Did you have to pull right up to the door?" she asked, embarrassed.

"Sorry, Punkin. I thought I was saving you some trouble." Lee Ann turned to glare at him.

"I mean, sorry, Lee Ann," he corrected himself. "Really though, try and have a great day. Just remember, if someone doesn't like you for who you are, they ain't worthy of your time anyway."

"Thanks, Dad." Although what he said seemed cliché, it did make her feel better as she looked up at the white slab of concrete that was the school building and the impersonal brown plastic letters that read, 'Pearson County High School'.

As soon as Lee Ann entered the hallway, she was struck by the number of boys wearing boots, cowboy and trucker hats, and other examples of what she and Hanna referred to as 'hickwear'. Numerous groups of girls glanced at her condescendingly before continuing their conversations.

It's best not to make eye contact with the unfriendly natives, she thought as she looked straight ahead toward the main office. Lee Ann must have looked out of place or slightly bewildered when she entered the room. She kept looking around her, unsure of where to go.

Just in front of her was a short, freckle-faced woman with a clownlike head of red, curly hair adorned in a classic school marm dress who seemed to Lee Ann to be an administrator.

"Excuse me. I'm new and I'm not sure where to go," Lee Ann admitted.

"Ah, you must be Lee Ann Daniels. Welcome to Pearson County High. I'm Mrs. Lamkins, your Assistant Principal. Here is your schedule. Please let me know if you need anythang."

"Sure, thanks," Lee Ann answered, trying hard not to laugh at her drawl that dominated every sentence she uttered.

· · ·

"Nice boots," a tall, blonde girl with a generous amount of makeup said to her as she passed through the hallway on the way to find the locker that she'd been assigned. Lee Ann was tempted to fire back at her about her caked on concealer, but she thought better of it, instead choosing to glare and shoot the girl a sarcastic smile. Once she reached her locker, she noticed a commotion just to her left. A plump girl with short, dark hair was focusing on opening her locker while two taller girls stood on either side of her.

"Well, Jenn, look what Katrina has on today, will ya?" A tall, thin redhead with teased hair pressed her hand flat against the locker, inches from Katrina's face.

"Looks like she raided my little brother's wardrobe, Lisa," Jenn answered, shifting her hips to one side sassily. Jenn had shoulder length brown hair and hazel eyes. Both of the girls wore short-sleeved shirts and cut-off jean shorts with cowboy boots. Lee Ann looked over at Katrina, thinking she was the only one at this school with any individuality or fashion sense. Katrina wore a black t-shirt under a red and black flannel shirt with a short, red tartan skirt and Converse All Stars.

"Your little brother usually wear skirts?" Lee Ann remarked.

Katrina giggled when Jenn and Lisa stared at Lee Ann as if she had spiders crawling from her ears.

"Who the hell are you?" Lisa hissed.

"Looks like the loser might have found herself a special friend," Jenn added, tauntingly.

"Maybe so. She does look pretty cute," Lee Ann said, looking Katrina up and down.

"Eww, she really is," Jenn gasped, walking away quickly, followed by Lisa. Both girls stopped for a second to look back at Lee Ann as if they expected her to try and kiss Katrina at any moment.

Lee Ann and Katrina exchanged a friendly glance and began to laugh.

"I'm not really into girls, by the way," Lee Ann revealed.

"Me neither. They just like to call me that because they're insecure, homophobic, and can't handle anyone with any individuality around here."

"I figured as much. Lee Ann's my name. I'm new," Lee Ann greeted, offering up her hand.

"I know. You kind of stand out like a sore thumb," Katrina observed. Immediately, Lee Ann noticed that Katrina did not have the usual southern accent that most of the other students had, although she couldn't quite place it.

Lee Ann looked around her as several groups of students looked away quickly to try and make it less obvious that they were staring. A group of boys continued to stare and talk among themselves, except for one who was trying to be a bit less obvious.

"Those boys are checking you out," Katrina noticed.

"Great, should I go up and ask them which one of them is going to take me to the hog calling contest?" Lee Ann asked. Katrina laughed. Lee Ann looked over at them again, noticing the shy one in the bunch had now dared to make eye contact with her. He was skinny and slumped a bit from bad posture. He had kind, brown eyes and dark hair with long bangs.

"Who's he?" Lee Ann inquired.

"Oh, David? You have a good eye. He's the only boy in that group that I can halfway stand," Katrina shared.

"I see."

"I don't think I've seen him so enthralled since Francine Wilkins came to the school."

"Who?"

"Oh, the last new girl we had here. She's tall and perfect like some kind of model. Not to take away from you. You could be a model, too," Katrina stated.

"Oh, stop it."

"No, really. You're one of those girls with natural beauty that doesn't even need makeup; you're tall and you've got a perfect figure, too, not to mention your eyes and your hair . . ."

"You're sure you're not into chicks?" They both laughed again.

The two of them struck up an immediate bond as they walked through the hallway comparing schedules.

"Oh cool, we have honors Spanish and Biology together," Katrina said with glee. Her round cheeks lit up. Lee Ann smiled at her and wondered how long Katrina had gone without a real friend.

Lee Ann sat through her morning classes, anticipating the chance to get to know her new friend. Finally, lunch arrived.

"So as the new girl what do I need to know?" Lee Ann asked as she and Katrina sat down at a lunch table by themselves in the far corner of the bustling cafeteria.

"Well, you might want to chill out with the hick jokes. They won't go over too well with this crowd," Katrina allowed.

"Which is something I noticed. Hate to sound like a yokel but you ain't from 'round here, are you?" Lee Ann put a fake emphasis on her southern drawl.

"Nope, I'm from Wisconsin. My father took a job managing a lumber mill and moved us here from Wausau, a slightly more civilized town with its own, eh, rural charm."

"That would explain your accent."

"What about you? I can't really tell that you have an accent, although it sneaks out from time to time."

"Yeah, I'm working on that, but I am from here. I just moved back from Nashville."

"Ugh, you escaped this place only to get thrust back into the fray?"

Lee Ann smiled, admiring the fact that her new friend seemed to have a much more unique way of expressing herself than other sixteen-year-olds.

"Yep. My mother recently passed away so I had to move in with my dad. They were divorced."

"I'm so sorry," Katrina said, putting a sympathetic hand on her shoulder. Lee Ann moved away a bit, not really being used to having physical contact with relative strangers.

"It's alright," Lee Ann replied, wanting to quickly change the subject.

"What happened?"

"Cancer," Lee Ann revealed, keeping her explanation short. Katrina looked into her eyes, sensing the pain and the resistance to offer up a detailed explanation. Lee Ann was spared another painful trip down memory lane by David's voice.

"Hello, I'm D . . . David," he stammered, sounding apprehensive as he approached their table.

"Hello David, I'm L . . . Lee Ann," she mimicked, making him laugh.

"Sorry, I'm a bit nervous about going up to people I don't know," he admitted in a guttural voice that sounded as if it might crack and go higher at any moment. His honesty was immediately refreshing to Lee Ann. She also couldn't help but think his spin on the southern accent was much cuter than the others. His slight drawl only revealed itself on his last word.

"Where you from, Lee Ann?" he inquired.

"Here, actually," she declared, watching his face wash in surprise.

"Really? Could have fooled me," he said, stunned.

"She just moved back from Nashville," Katrina explained.

"I see. I've been there a few times. My dad loves the Grand Ole Opry. I don't know, it's kind of boring. Memphis, now there's a city with character," he expressed.

"Never been, but I hope to get out of Tennessee once and for all someday," she said.

"Sounds like a worthy goal. After all, there's a whole world out there," he sat down beside her.

"Well, just make yourself at home, then," Katrina uttered sarcastically.

"Oh sorry, can I join ya?"

"Of course," Lee Ann looked over at Katrina to make sure she hadn't upset her new friend. Katrina gave David a slight eye roll.

"I guess," Katrina sighed.

"Great!" David said. His friends kept looking over from a nearby table in disbelief that he had stayed at the freak-girl table for so long.

"So David, what do you like to do for fun?" Lee Ann said, bracing herself for the usual praise of hunting or mudding.

"I like to go up to Widow's Bluff just before sunset and watch the barges go down the river." Katrina looked at him slyly, suspicious that he was giving the kind of answer a girl would want to hear.

"I love Widow's Bluff," Lee Ann exclaimed.

"You do?" David said, sounding genuinely surprised. Katrina, however, was still skeptical of his motives.

"And just how often do you go up there, David?" Katrina asked.

"Oh, I don't know at least once every couple of weeks. I don't just go hiking there, I like Rutherford Landing and Meriwether Lewis Park as well."

"Me too," Lee Ann proclaimed. Katrina just shook her head and went back to her mashed potatoes.

"David, come over here, dude!" one of David's friends called out.

"Yeah, your time is up at the freak table!" crowed another one, followed by laughter. Katrina shot them a glare they wouldn't soon forget.

"Gotta go, but I'll see you around. Maybe we can climb up to Widow's Bluff sometime soon." David smiled, locking eyes with Lee Ann for a long moment.

"Sure, I don't see why not," Lee Ann responded, feeling much better about her new situation. For the first time in quite a while, she was starting to open up and feel like her old self again.

"He's kind of cute," Lee Ann said.

"I guess so. His choice of friends makes me question his character, but he is definitely the nice one in the bunch," Katrina said. "Oh no," she said suddenly, looking over toward the cafeteria entrance.

"What is it?" Lee Ann asked.

"A subhuman specimen known as Mary Hartford," Katrina practically moaned.

Lee Ann gazed at what looked to her to be a full-sized country version of a Barbie doll. Mary had long, perfect blonde hair that spilled around her shoulders, a short-sleeved white tank top, apple bottom jeans, and red cowboy boots. Behind her were the two other girls she'd encountered earlier.

"Look away, don't draw their gaze," Katrina said.

"What? I'm not afraid of some over-dressed Barbie doll," Lee Ann proclaimed.

Mary happened to be looking right in Lee Ann's direction and began to walk toward their table.

"Oh no, 'it' and her two psycho sidekicks are coming this way. Ugh!" Katrina protested, referring to Lisa and Jenn.

"Well, well, look who found a friend, girls," Mary teased, standing right beside Lee Ann.

"What do you want, Mary?" Katrina asked.

"Oh, the same thing I always want, dear. I want to know why you are such a fat loser," Mary stated nonchalantly. Lee Ann immediately stood up, crossed her arms and looked Mary in the eye, being about the same height. It seemed to shock Mary because she was taller than most of the girls in her grade.

"What do you think you're doing, freak?" Mary crossed her arms. "Look, new chick or whatever you are, I do and say whatever I want. You are new so I'll cut you some slack, but you had better learn your place around here."

"Oh, excuse me, no one made me aware of the phony hierarchy you've created," Lee Ann shot back, unmoved or intimidated. Mary looked confused by her words.

"It means I'm not keen on following your rules," Lee Ann explained.

Mary did not answer right away. It was clear that she wasn't used to someone standing up to her.

"What's the matter? Was I not clear enough with my explanation?" Lee Ann added.

"Look, you may think you're hot stuff, but I will take you down a notch or two if you don't learn your place!" Mary threatened. Her friends moved in closer behind her, making her feel much less intimidated.

Lee Ann laughed. "It's going to take more than the three of you. Who else is a member of your Army of Barbies?" Lee Ann commented while Katrina watched, dumbfounded. She had never witnessed anyone stand up to Mary like that.

"Just remember what I said. It might save your life one day. See you around. Come on girls, we have better things to do with our time than talk to freaks and fatties," she declared, turning away from Lee Ann.

"Wow, I am so impressed! You are my hero!" Katrina exclaimed.

Lee Ann sat back down and took a deep breath. The table where

David sat noticed what had transpired, too. Lee Ann thought she over-heard the words, 'tough girl,' which made her smile.

"It was nothing. Look, you shouldn't let her treat you that way. You could probably take her down if push came to shove," Lee Ann encouraged.

"I will be the first to admit that I'm not a fighter," Katrina said, making ridges in her mashed potatoes with her fork.

"Neither am I," Lee Ann said.

"What? Could have fooled me. I thought you were going to start mopping the floor with her at any moment."

Lee Ann laughed, feeling better than she had in many a day. For a while, she even forgot the tremendous loss that felt like a heavy weight on her chest.

CHAPTER 4
THE WIND SPEAKS

S hirley finished washing the dishes and looked out the window that faced the backyard. She shook her head as her eyes found her stepdaughter's figure squatted on the rocks just inside the woods.

"Why does she spend so much time out there?" Shirley asked Charles as he came in the front door and hung his jacket on the hook just inside the door.

"She has always loved the outdoors. Won't get her within miles of a mall, but ask her to go on a hike and her eyes just light right up."

"Charles, that's not normal," she insisted, turning to bat her long eyelashes at him.

"What's normal, Shirl? Come on, she's her own person. I love her for that," he said.

"Well, you are always telling me I should make more of an effort to get to know her, but she's so closed off to me."

"What do you mean?"

"Every time I try and strike up a conversation it goes nowhere. We just don't have much in common. I would love to take her shopping or something but she would never go with me."

Charles laughed and shook his head.

"What?" she asked.

"You got to try and do something she likes to do, even if you don't exactly enjoy it," he said.

"I'll give it a try, but not right now. These potatoes ain't gonna cook themselves, and you sure ain't gonna cook 'em," she said, looking at him over her shoulder with a wink.

"Now come on, Shirl, I just cooked us some steaks the other night," he insisted.

"Yeah, if it's on the grill you'll cook it I guess," she teased him as he turned to get a coke out of the refrigerator.

Lee Ann was busy sketching a different section of the spring creek than she had during previous efforts. The wind rustled the leaves around her, blowing through her hair as she stopped to look at what she had just drawn. Quickly bored with it, she turned the page to sketch the faces of her newfound friends. Her artistry had always been therapeutic, but as of late it was just about the only thing that would soothe her when her grief for her mother was too much to bear.

She began to draw Katrina's friendly eyes, pink cheeks, and generous smile, completing her figure in a standing position. Next, she sketched David's shy, but friendly eyes, his smiling face, and dark etchings for his bangs that fell into his eyes. The afternoon was long over and she was trying to sketch in the dying light of the day.

The calls of birds began to cease, replaced by a cascade of chirps from crickets. Lee Ann lay against a tree and slipped into a nap. After a short while, she awoke in the gathering darkness and gazed off through the eastern portion of the woods. It was then she heard a thin, distant sound that was almost human in origin. The sound seemed to carry off as if it were the wind itself making utterances.

She placed the sketchbook back in her satchel and stood up to observe the direction of the noise more intently, unable to make out much in the gloom. Without thinking, she switched on the flashlight on her cell phone, hopped over the creek, and began to walk through the woods towards the eastern border of their property, rustling and crunching leaves as she went. She paused for an instant, having heard the sound again, a bit closer now, though still some distance off. It sounded like words that couldn't quite fully form, feminine in nature.

Lee Ann's eyes were now wide and the slight chill in the air sent a shiver that traveled up her back. Curiosity drove her on for another quarter of a mile where the trees began to get larger and more ancient. At the very edge of the property line was a pink surveyor's ribbon tied to the lower limbs of an oak and a diamond-shaped sign bolted to the tree that read, 'Safety Zone, No Hunting, Tennessee Wildlife Resources Management.' Lee Ann wanted to explore this area, so she advanced past the marker into the dense woods.

The terrain immediately became steep and rocky. Making it to the crest of the rise, Lee Ann stopped to survey the land in front of her. The daylight had faded completely; the multi-color sun had long since retreated behind the distant hills. The hills, which stacked up one behind the other, seemed to go on forever. The darkness cast a gloom over the unending rows of bony fingers of bare branches that reached for the sky. Just when she was ready to turn back, she heard the sound again, much closer this time.

"He—" it seemed to say. It was most definitely a voice this time and could no longer be mistaken for the wind, but who would be out here at this hour, wandering about making incoherent mutterings?

The thought sent another chill up Lee Ann's back.

What if someone needs help? She asked herself, suddenly striking down the other side of the hill. At the bottom was a dry creek bed that had been hidden by vegetation from the top of the hill. She did not like how it was darker down here in the hollow. There was a movement that rustled the leaves about a hundred yards to her north that made her turn abruptly toward the sound. In the fading light, she couldn't see anything other than the relentless maze of tree trunks.

"HeeelP!" the voice spoke again, about a yard from the rustling. For the first time, Lee Ann could make out an actual word from the mutterings. It was unmistakably the voice of a woman.

The quality of the voice sounded altered as if run through an effects loop with an overabundance of reverb. It could have been uttered in a large chamber or a cave the way it echoed and ended suddenly.

Lee Ann stared at the origin of the sound in disbelief, her teeth chattering. She still could not see any sign of life among the trees. The temperature of the air around her dropped unnaturally. Unless the figure was hiding behind the trees, it should have been visible at such close proximity, but no one stepped forward. She felt a tingle in her hands.

That's freaking odd.

"Help ME!" it said. The sound was only a few feet away now. There was no one there to stir the decaying foliage of the forest floor like there should have been; no sound of footsteps in the dry leaves.

Lee Ann let out a yell of alarm. Without thinking, she turned and ran back up the hill, operating on pure fight-or-flight instinct.

After she made it to the top, she caught her breath and looked back behind her, frightfully expecting to see a woman climbing the slope behind her. However, there was no one there and no figure stirred in the hollow below.

Shaking her head, Lee Ann turned and ran all the way past the boundary of the Wildlife Management area, jumped over the small creek and ran through the darkening garden toward the back door.

Shirley saw Lee Ann's expression; her eyes widened. She opened the back door.

"What's goin' on out there? Did you get spooked in the woods?"

Lee Ann took a moment to catch her breath, shifting her gaze from Shirley's face over to her astonished father who sat leaning on the counter with one hand on his coke.

"You okay, hun?" Charles asked.

"Yes," Lee Ann said, catching her breath. "I just got turned around and it frightened me because it had gotten dark."

"That's why you cried out? Are you sure that's all it was?" Shirley asked.

"Yes, I'm okay. Just scared me for a minute. I'm fine, really," she said, flashing a smile before heading for the stairs. Charles and Shirley looked at each other; Charles shrugged and took another swig of his soda.

Lee Ann closed her bedroom door and stared out of her window at the dim garden and the woods behind it, shrouded in darkness. She wondered if she'd done the right thing by not mentioning the voice.

Had they not heard it before themselves? It didn't seem as if they had, but they had heard her yell. This unsettled her.

Lee Ann reached up and turned on the overhead light in addition to the bedside lamp that was already on. She was hoping the extra light would lend her some comfort, but she still felt unnerved.

Surely, if there was someone out there they would have wandered into their garden by now seeking help, but no figure appeared.

Charles knocked on the door, startling Lee Ann.

"Come in," she said, taking a deep breath.

"What happened out there?" Charles inquired.

"Nothing. I thought I heard something that's all. Maybe it was just an owl or something," she said trying to convince herself as much as him.

"Oh, I see," he responded as he sat down on the bed and patted her shoulder.

"Maybe it's part of the grievin' process, hearin' things, that is," Charles offered. Lee Ann looked over at him, creasing her forehead.

"Maybe." Lee Ann's thoughts shifted suddenly toward her mother. She looked at the assortment of necklaces her mother had given her hanging from her mirror along with the assorted photos along the bottom, a shrine to her mother that had been recreated the same way it had been arranged at her old house. "I miss her so much, Dad," she said as tears began to flow. The sight of his concerned eyes had been too much for her. She cried on her father's shoulders as he put his arms around her, hugging her tightly.

"I know you do, hun. You're gonna be alright," he urged.

They sat there in their embrace for several minutes until Shirley's call from downstairs broke the silence,

"Dinner's ready!"

The next day at school, Lee Ann walked directly to Katrina's locker. She was happy to find her friend getting her books for the first two periods of the day.

"What's up?" Katrina asked, looking at Lee Ann's expression.

"I want to tell you about something odd that happened last night."

"Sure! Fire away! I'm a connoisseur of all things weird. Well, most things anyway," said Katrina, obviously excited that her new friend would confide in her.

Lee Ann looked back and forth to see if anyone would overhear; seeing no one near, she began to recount the evening before.

"I heard a voice in the woods, coming from the wildlife area that borders our land. I went over there to investigate and there was no one there. I kept hearing the voice only a few feet away from me. I should have been able to spot someone at that distance, even in the fading light, but no one was there."

"That's weird!" Katrina was enthralled.

"Not too weird. Other people have heard and seen things in that area," David suddenly said, appearing right behind Katrina.

"Where did you come from, eavesdropper?" Katrina asked.

"Sorry, couldn't help but overhear. Where is your property, Lee Ann?" David asked, matter-of-factly.

"Don't tell him if you don't want to, Lee Ann. That's confidential info and it's none of his business," Katrina insisted.

"I'm only asking because if you live close to the Wildlife Management Area, that's where Thief's Hollow is."

"What's that?" Katrina asked.

"You mean you haven't heard?" David looked at Katrina and then over to Lee Ann.

"Heard what?" Lee Ann asked.

"Are you sure you're from here?"

"I told you, I grew up in Nashville."

"Well, the area that's now a wildlife preserve was supposedly some kind of colony back in the forties or so I believe. There's another belief that it was a hideout for some thieves, hence the name."

"Colony?" Lee Ann asked.

"Colony or commune of some kind. No one knows for sure what they were doing there or who they were, but they were murdered," he revealed.

"Murdered? As in killed in cold blood?" Katrina asked.

"Yep, that's all I know about the history behind it. Older people are pretty tight-lipped if you ask 'em 'cuz they believe in the thieves story. If they know more than they're letting on, they don't tell it," David allowed.

"Ok, that's mysterious," Lee Ann said. "Where EXACTLY is this hollow where the colony was located?"

"It's on the western side of the preserve. I could show you on a map. Anyway, people don't go there very often except the parts where you can hunt. Supposedly, there's a lot of wildlife, but no one stays anywhere close to nightfall," David shared.

"So, it's haunted then?" Katrina asked. As soon as she said this, Lee Ann looked at her as if she were voicing a thought she herself was suppressing.

"Something like that," he answered.

"But why do they think that? There has to be some factual basis for it," Katrina continued with her line of inquiry.

"People have heard voices and stuff. Like I said, it's just rumors. Who knows if any of it's real," David said, trying to reassure Lee Ann, who was visibly a bit shaken.

"You said they've seen things too. What kinds of things?" Lee Ann asked.

"I don't know . . . something about orbs and even figures being seen and voices being heard in the woods. I'm not sure," he said.

"Well you are just so specific in your descriptions, aren't you?" Katrina complained.

"Sorry, that's all I know."

"Do you know anyone that's actually seen or heard any of these things?" Lee Ann questioned.

"Well, I know you, don't I?" David said as he looked up at the clock and realized the late bell was about to sound. "Got to go, I can't be late to Mrs. Wilburn's class again," he said.

Lee Ann leaned against the lockers and stared into space.

"Don't let that bother you. It's just a story, right? People believe in all kinds of things that aren't real: mirages, hallucinations. Not that I'm implying that you were hallucinating," Katrina clarified as she came over and rubbed Lee Ann's arm gently.

"It seemed so real last night; the voice that is," Lee Ann insisted.

"Hearing voices are we?" Mary's voice interjected mockingly from behind her.

Lee Ann turned around to face her with a scowl that could freeze the blood.

"None of your business!" Katrina said.

"Who asked you, fatty?" Mary shouted at Katrina. Jenn was standing just behind Mary to back her up, if need be.

Katrina's face began to glow red with anger. They had used this name to describe her many times, but this appeared to be one time too many.

"Take that back, you painted neanderthal," Katrina said, moving past Lee Ann until she was right in front of Mary. Jenn took a step forward, crossing her arms menacingly.

Mary feigned a laugh.

"Ha, not a chance, fatty!" she said pushing her so hard Katrina lost her footing and fell squarely on her behind. Lee Ann's eyes narrowed to two fiery slits.

"Take it BACK!" Lee Ann shouted as Katrina got back up, dusted herself off and stepped up beside her, glaring at Mary.

"Not a chance, freaks!" Mary cajoled.

Without thinking, Lee Ann grabbed Mary's blouse and slammed her back against the locker while several students gathered around to watch. Katrina got behind Lee Ann. Jenn seemed momentarily perplexed, unable to challenge Lee Ann in her wrath.

"What's going on here?" Mrs. Lamkins asked, suddenly appearing behind Lee Ann.

"Ms. Daniels, let go of Ms. Hartford this instant!" she insisted. Mr. Harris, the principal, began to run awkwardly in their direction from the office. He had lost his leg in the Vietnam War and had been outfitted with an artificial limb; when he moved, he dragged his right leg.

Lee Ann took her hand off Mary's shirt and stepped backward, flaring her nostrils.

Mary turned toward Mrs. Lamkins, exuding outrage.

"Now, what's this all about?" Mrs. Lamkins asked as Mr. Harris appeared to her right, his hands on his hips.

"I was minding my own business when she slammed me against the lockers," Mary said.

"Not true," Katrina interjected.

"Hold on, Ms. Friedman, allow Ms. Hartford to finish her account of things," Mr. Harris insisted.

Lee Ann shook her head, thinking it ridiculous how he insisted on calling all of the students by their last names.

"I was having a conversation with Katrina when Lee Ann came over and shoved me hard against the locker and threatened me," Mary explained.

"Is that true?" Mrs. Lamkins asked Lee Ann.

"No, not all of it. She . . ."

"Did you shove her against the locker and threaten her?" Mr. Harris asked.

"I shoved her, but only after she . . ."

"Come with me to the office, Ms. Daniels," Mrs. Lamkins insisted.

"But aren't you going to listen to her side of the story?" Katrina asked, incredulously.

"She can tell us her side in the office!" Mrs. Lamkins said. Mary shot a sarcastic smile at Lee Ann as she was led away. Katrina turned toward Mary and Jenn for an angry retort, but they had already scampered down the hallway just as the bell rang.

"What about Mary? Shouldn't she be going to the office, too?" Katrina shouted down the hallway.

Lee Ann plopped herself down in the chair in front of Mrs. Lamkins' desk and folded her arms.

Mrs. Lamkins grabbed a couple of forms from behind her desk and pulled a pen out from behind her ear. She sat perfectly straight at her desk, as if she had a poll attached to her back, and folded her hands together on the desk in front of her.

"Now, Ms. Daniels, you are new here, which is why I'm only going to suspend you for a day so that you can think of a better way to resolve your differences with your fellow students."

Lee Ann's forehead creased in disapproval. "You're going to suspend me without hearing what I have to say? That is preposterous! Mary Hartford came up and called Katrina a fatty. When Katrina asked her to apologize, Mary shoved her so hard she fell to the floor! I was just trying to help my friend, Mrs. Lamkins. Mary bullies Katrina all the time!"

"Well, we will call Ms. Hartford in to see if that's true," she replied.

"What about Katrina?" Lee Ann asked, but Mrs. Lamkins got up and left the office as if the matter were closed for discussion. A few minutes later, Mrs. Lamkins came back into the office with Mary just behind her.

"Now, Ms. Hartsford, Ms. Daniels says you pushed Ms. Friedman. Is that true?"

"No, she's lying."

Lee Ann's mouth fell open and her eyebrows folded inwards.

"You're the liar!" Lee Ann shot back.

"Girls that's enough. Thank you, Ms. Hartford. You may go back to class," Mrs. Lamkins said.

"You're not going to suspend her? This is outrageous!" Lee Ann exclaimed. It was clear that Mrs. Lamkins wasn't interested in hearing her cries of righteous indignation.

"If you are going to stay at Pearson County High School you will have to learn to get along with other girls in a more constructive way and learn to control your anger. We don't handle disputes here in a violent manner. I'm going to call your father," Mrs. Lamkins said as Lee Ann sighed loudly, shook her head, and turned sideways in her chair, too angry to even look at the vice principal.

CHAPTER 5
TALL TALES AND CAMPFIRE STORIES

Lee Ann took her time walking home, knowing that she had an uncomfortable confrontation waiting for her once she got there. Normally, this was the part of the day that she enjoyed. For the most part, it was a time of solitude, except for the occasional vehicle roaring by. She relished the feeling of the sun on her skin and the quiet beauty of the woods that met the road most of the way home. The Franklins' place was the only other inhabited dwelling along their stretch of Green Creek Road and it was almost a mile away. This remote quality was something that Lee Ann loved yet found dismal at the same time.

She pulled out her phone and noticed the dreaded text from her father.

Got a call from your principal. Come straight home so we can talk about this.

Fighting? What were you thinking?

Lee Ann rolled her eyes, put the phone back in her pocket without responding, and wondered if her father would take the school's side or her own. She didn't have long to find out.

Despite all the drama originating from her defense of her friend, Lee Ann's thoughts were more concerned with the mystery of the colony David spoke about and the voice she had heard. If nothing else, it allowed her to hold out hope that what she'd experienced was not the overworked imagination of a girl suffering from grief, but a possible encounter with the supernatural. She pondered the possibility that some restless spirit was reaching out to her, that she might possess some gift to bridge the world of the living and the dead. The more she thought about this, the more that explanation seemed almost as unsettling. She planned to see if her father knew anything and if so, why he kept it from her.

Charles was pacing back and forth in front of the window, smoking a cigarette. The sight of this made Lee Ann that much more nervous because she knew he had been trying to quit and hadn't smoked around her in quite some time. When he caught sight of her approaching the house, he quickly stubbed out his cigarette into an ashtray on the kitchen table and walked toward the door.

Lee Ann took a deep breath and pushed the door open.

"Well?" Charles frowned and crossed his arms. Something about the whole scene seemed comical to Lee Ann. Maybe it was the absurdity of people being angry with her for doing what she thought was the right thing at the time. Maybe it was the way her father always rolled up his sleeves and wore a vest, jacket, and several layers even when it wasn't very cold outside.

"Somethin' funny?"

"No, sorry, Dad. Please, just let me tell you exactly what happened."

Charles went into the den and huffed for Lee Ann to follow.

"I'm listenin'," he said as he sat down in the dark brown armchair, motioning for her to sit on the opposite couch.

Lee Ann took off her button-covered jean jacket and flung it on the couch.

"Now, you know Shirley likes all the coats hung up right away," he reminded her.

"Got it," Lee Ann answered quickly, not wanting to fan the flames of his anger.

She hung up the jacket and swiftly returned to her seat on the couch.

"Every day at school those girls bully Katrina and she is the nicest, coolest girl you'll ever meet," she stated. Charles leaned in and nodded.

"Today, Mary Hartford and that terrible shrew, Jenn Ledbetter came up and butted into our conversation. When Katrina told her it was none of her business, she called Katrina a fatty and pushed her to the ground." Lee Ann paused to gauge his reaction so far. His bushy brows were folded in, his mouth tight.

"Go on," he said.

"Well, I told her to take it back—calling Katrina a fatty—and she refused. So, I shoved her up against the locker."

"That's where you took a wrong turn. You know that's not the way to settle things."

"You sound just like the principal," she retorted.

"I'm sorry, but she's right, hun."

"But you and Mom both said that sometimes it's necessary to fight for what's right."

"Yeah, but this wasn't a situation where it was called for. Katrina is going to have to learn to defend herself," he insisted.

"Against two or three girls?"

"I do see your point, but shouldn't you have handled it differently?"

"I'm sorry, Dad. I know I'm supposed to confess that I did something wrong and talk about how I'll handle it differently, but I don't think I did anything wrong."

Charles was genuinely astonished, but also somewhat proud of her response. At that moment she reminded him of his younger self—stubborn and self-righteous—and of his ex-wife, who had exhibited the same traits, which provided the initial attractive spark between them.

"Dad, she needed to be put in her place. I didn't hurt her. I just showed her that we weren't going to be pushed around. Look, I know she didn't threaten me directly but Mom always taught me to protect the people that are important to me and do what I think is best."

"Well, she was right about that, too." Charles was a bit flustered, not wanting to seem like his daughter had won the argument, especially after having gotten in trouble.

"You're still grounded, though. Even if you did what you thought was right you still broke a school rule. There are consequences for that," he said.

"Is that your idea or one of Shirley's?" Lee Ann asked, regretting saying it as soon as it left her lips.

Charles rose to his feet and flared his nostrils.

"I'm sorry, Dad, I was out of line there. I didn't mean that. I just noticed that sometimes she runs all over you and you don't stand up for yourself."

He sat back down and put his head between his knees for a moment and scratched his head. Looking back up into his daughter's eyes, he took a deep breath.

"Tomorrow I'm going up there to talk to Mrs. Lamkins and Mr. Harris about these girls. If they are going around bullying girls at your school somethin's got to be done about it."

"Dad, no. It will just make things worse. They will just want to retaliate against us for ratting them out," she insisted.

"My decision on this is final. Now, go on up to your room until I decide on the particulars of your groundin'," he said, locking his fingers together under his mouth.

Lee Ann sighed, got up, and ran for the stairs.

"And no phone," he added.

She paused on the front stair, took out her cell phone, laid in on the bannister and continued her ascent up the steps. Throwing herself on the bed, she fell asleep within minutes, overcome by the emotional and physical exhaustion of the day. She thought of her mother and how she would have probably defended her decision to look out for her friend. Feelings of loss and despair lingered on the edges of this thought, but fatigue took over, covering her in a comforting veil of sleep.

When she awoke hours later, she looked out the window. The late afternoon shadows were being overtaken by a more complete darkness, leaking into the garden, which was now partially cleared of vines from her father's work on it the previous weekend. Her eyes were then drawn to the woods on the far right that bordered on the wildlife preserve. Although it could have easily been in her head, she swore she heard the voice again, high and shrill off in the distance.

"Help!" It was plaintive and sad at first, but increasingly panicked during the second utterance. The third time it was undoubtedly a scream.

"HELP!!!"

Lee Ann sprung to her feet and slipped on her Vans. Her descent down the stairs and across the house happened so quickly, Lee Ann practically turned off all cognizance as if she were in a total, single-minded trance. Before she could see her father's response to her leaving the house, she was through the door and across the garden. The growing darkness from the woods seemed to be advancing like a dark cloak was about to be thrown over the house.

"HELP ME!" The voice called out again, closer this time, and followed by the unmistakable sound of a gunshot—or was it multiple gunshots? There might have been another voice in there, higher in register.

Lee Ann paused, thinking of the foolishness of running into a situation where she could be potentially shot, but something drove her on through the tangled thorns and brambles of the woods, despite potential danger. By the time she made it to the edge of the preserve, the darkness was complete. She ventured over the hill, into the hollow she'd previously visited, and onto the next hill beyond that. After descending the rocky hillside, she followed what seemed to be a cleared footpath that led like a tunnel between adjacent hills. Despite the near total darkness, Lee Ann pressed on as if she'd been this way before, her flashlight guiding her.

The silhouette of two buildings ahead stopped her in her tracks. One of them appeared more sturdy and newer than the other. Lee Ann guessed the newer, larger structure was a house and the other a barn of some sort, although it was too far away for her to be sure. Her gaze shifted as something stirred in the leaves on the forest floor. Someone or something was clearly slumped over on its stomach just a few yards to her right, stirring the leaves with kicking feet.

Lee Ann put her hand to her mouth as she drew closer. There was another sound, like someone running through the forest. Lee Ann thought of the gunshots and ducked behind a tree. From there she peered into the gloom but could not find the source of the footsteps.

Looking over at the figure on the ground, which Lee Ann was much closer to now, she realized it was a woman in a nightgown who had stopped moving.

The sound of footsteps in the leaves had ceased, and Lee Ann got back up to head toward the woman to see if she could help her. As she reached the woman, she was close enough to see a spot of blood on her side. The woman's hands were obscured within the leaves and her features shrouded by the dark, curly locks of her hair.

You can help them. You must! The voice in Lee Ann's head was comforting, yet insistent. There was also something strangely familiar about it, although she couldn't match the voice with anyone she knew.

"HELP!" the shrill voice yelled again as someone grabbed Lee Ann's arm from behind.

Lee Ann whirled around and looked into the face of a girl, also in a nightgown. Her face, almost as pale white as her attire, was wide-eyed with fear.

Lee Ann screamed at the sight of her, sitting straight up in her bed afterward.

"What the . . ." she said, feeling disoriented as she rubbed her eyes to make sure she was really awake this time.

She jumped up and went immediately to the window.

The garden and woods were bathed in twilight, not in darkness as it was in her dream. She took a deep breath and went back to sit on the edge of her bed; she needed to pull herself back into the present and get a handle on the meaning of it all.

Over dinner, Lee Ann was quiet and lost in her thoughts—mainly because she was mulling over everything that was happening, but also to avoid talking about the day's event with Shirley. Shirley looked at her almost as if she could sense this.

"So, I understand you got in trouble at school today," Shirley said, her face stoic and serious.

"Yes, we had it out already. Lee Ann is grounded," Charles explained, smiling softly at his daughter. Lee Ann smiled at her father's efforts to save her from another lecture.

"Well, I certainly hope you learned your lesson. I used to know girls who fought a lot growing up, and I think at least one of them is now in jail."

"She doesn't fight a lot. This is the first time she's ever been in one," Charles interjected.

"I know, dear, but we don't want this to lead to a pattern. Besides, the Hartfords are a pretty upstanding family. You don't want to become known for roughing up John Hartford's daughter," she chided. Lee Ann's eyes widened as she looked at Shirley.

So that's it then? You're worried about your reputation.

Lee Ann looked over at her father and changed the subject, not wanting to hear what her stepmother might say next.

"So, Dad, what do you know about a haunted hollow?" she asked, swearing she heard his fork clang loudly against his plate like he'd dropped it.

"Haunted hollow?" he asked.

"Yeah. David, a boy at school, says that there is a place inside the wildlife preserve next door that is haunted; that only hunters go there and no one goes after dark."

"No one goes after dark 'cause it's a remote place and it's illegal to hunt there at night," he insisted.

"So there's no legend about a colony that lived there?" she inquired. Charles and Shirley's eyes met when she said this.

"So there is?" she asked.

"Ok, so there is something that happened out there," Charles finally admitted.

"What happened?"

"Well, there wasn't a colony. It was a group of thieves," he said.

"David says many believe there was some kind of colony out there," Lee Ann said, thinking aloud.

"Maybe he's heard a different version of the story, but that's the way I heard it. Some thieves that had been robbing banks in the area— they even murdered someone in town," He picked up his fork, ready to resume eating again.

"Why is it so hard to believe there could be a group of thieves or a colony in the woods or whatever?" she wondered.

"That's not the part that's hard to believe, dear," Shirley chimed in. "It's the stories you hear about voices and people in the woods."

"Aha, so it's true! People think it's haunted," Lee Ann declared.

"Again, tall tales and campfire stories. They used to tell that one at the Boy Scouts camp over in Hohenwald when I was growin' up," Charles said with a grin.

"So what happened to these thieves?" Lee Ann inquired.

"Well, it's pretty commonly known in these parts. According to the story, the thieves took up in a hideout way back in what later came to be known as Thief's Hollow after committin' all sorts of robberies in the area. Like I said, they killed someone in town. I believe they killed the wife of a prominent man. I guess they were probably breakin' in cuz they knew he had money. Once they found the location of the thieves' camp, there was a shootout in the dead of night between the Laverne sheriff and his men and the thieves," he said.

"Who won?" Lee Ann asked as she leaned in, propping up her chin with her fist.

"Police did, I reckon. None of the thieves made it out alive."

"I see. So there must be stories about it from the papers back in the forties," she declared.

"I'm sure there are," Charles answered.

"So why haven't you ever told me about any of that?" Lee Ann asked.

Charles sighed, looked over at Shirley and then back to Lee Ann.

"I don't know, I guess I didn't want you to be scared of the stories. I was tryin' to protect you, I reckon."

"Well, I'm sixteen now. I think I'm old enough to hear it," she insisted.

"I certainly don't want you to be afraid of the woods as much as you love 'em," he went on.

"Don't worry," she said. For a moment, she thought about bringing up the issue of the voices she'd heard and the dream she'd had, but as she looked up at Shirley's condescending eyes staring at her, she thought better of it.

CHAPTER 6
A PIECE OF THE PUZZLE

Lee Ann's alarm screeched in her ear like it did every morning. For one brief instant, she sat up, thinking she needed to get ready. Then the events of the day before slowly played back in her mind and reminded her that she was suspended. Shortly after closing her eyes, she heard the footsteps of her father and heard the faint voice of her stepmother just behind him.

"She needs to get up like the rest of us, anyway."

Lee Ann sat up and sighed, knowing that Charles would be knocking on the door and entering the room at any moment. The familiar knock came soon enough.

"Come in, Dad," Lee Ann's voice was listless and tired, with more than a hint of sarcasm and ennui.

"How'd you know it was me?" he joked.

"Oh, I don't know, because it's always you," she said, pulling her long bangs out of her eyes.

"Now, Shirley and I feel that you need to go on and get up to make the most of your day. I'm taking your computer, but I'll leave you your cell phone in case of an emergency. You need to promise me you won't surf the net all day," he said. Lee Ann raised an eyebrow and sighed.

"Dad, the internet connection here isn't even that good on the best of days."

"Good, I want you to do whatever work you can for school so you don't get behind," he said.

"Well, all I had to do is my homework, which I've already done," she pointed out. "I'll text Katrina and get her to send me the assignments for tonight."

"Good plan. I can always count on you to get your work done," he said with a smile. Just behind him, Shirley peered through the cracked door of the bedroom. Charles' peripheral vision spotted her and his tone changed suddenly.

"However, that doesn't mean I condone your behavior as of late. You need to reflect on it and see if you can figure out how to get along with those girls. Maybe even apologize," he added.

"That will be the day. Ok, how about this, Dad: if Mary agrees to apologize to Katrina, I'll apologize to her."

"Lee . . ," her dad tried his best stern voice , "I just want you to think about it. At the very least, don't go out of your way to get into conflicts with them."

Lee Ann nodded perfunctorily, pulled the bedspread off of her legs, and threw her feet over the side. She gave her father a half-hearted smile and her gaze drifted off toward the forest behind the house.

"You alright, Punkin?" he asked, his guys glassy with concern.

"I'm okay," she said, thinking about how her mother would have responded to the situation at school.

If that girl has been bullying your friend all this time, she needs to be put in her place. It's time people stood up to her, Lee Ann imagined her mother saying.

"Have a good day, sweetie," Charles said just before leaving the room.

Lee Ann breathed in deeply, putting her hands to her temples to push back against another flood of memories about her mother.

Lee Ann went downstairs to eat breakfast. As she sat in the kitchen stabbing a piece of waffle, she pondered everything she'd heard about the legend, along with what she'd seen in the dream and the unmistakable voice she'd heard in the woods.

Is the dream a product of my mind trying to put this whole thing together—filling in the pieces with my imagination, or am I being given a glimpse of things that did actually happen?

A sudden rap at the kitchen door startled Lee Ann, causing her to jump slightly. It was David, standing sheepishly and peering through the storm door.

"Hey! I couldn't let you spend your suspension all alone. I thought I'd come to cheer you up," he said. Lee Ann rolled her eyes, smiled, and walked over to the door.

"Do you always just show up unannounced?" she said, not opening the door for him at first.

"Only on occasion," he insisted with a smile.

Something about his manner and friendly smile caused her to open the door and let him inside.

"You scared me."

"Sorry, I'll ring the doorbell next time. I just saw you through the window."

"Do you want a waffle?" she asked him.

"Sure, why not," he said. His eyes followed her as she went over to the toaster oven and put a waffle on a small plate and applied butter to it.

"So, do you maybe wanna go and check out the hollow?" he asked as she put the waffle down in front of him.

Lee Ann didn't respond right away as she thought about the voice and the dream again.

"It's daytime and all, so we shouldn't have to worry about well, you know," he said, as if sensing her thoughts.

"Sure," she answered confidently.

"Great," he said, his mouth full of waffle. "They're all talking about you, you know."

"Oh? What are they saying?"

"Most think you're cool for standing up to Mary. She treats a lot of people like garbage if they don't meet her standards. The only people that have a problem with what you've done is Mary's closest friends."

Lee Ann smiled, feeling satisfied.

"Cool, I guess it's about time that someone stood up to her." Lee

Ann sighed and looked off through the window toward the woods. "Look, David. I'm going to tell you about something else, but you have to promise not to tell anyone," she confided.

"Sure, I'm all ears," he replied, leaning in.

"I had a dream where I heard voices similar to the ones I heard in the wildlife preserve, and I saw . . ." Lee Ann gulped, thinking of how real the dream seemed. "I . . .saw a woman who'd been shot and a girl that was trying to get away."

"Get away from who?" David said, leaning in more as he swallowed a huge bite of waffle.

"I don't know. Whoever had the gun," she responded, trembling now. "There was also this voice telling me that I needed to help them. I don't know how to explain it exactly, but the voice seemed familiar even though I can't figure out who it was."

"Whoa, that's pretty strange, but it is, after all, just a dream," he said, putting a reassuring hand on her arm.

"I don't know," she said hesitantly.

"What do you mean?"

"What if it's all connected—all of the things that have been happening? What if I'm being given the pieces of a puzzle?" Lee Ann was overcome by a sense of intuition. Having voiced her thoughts, her confidence about this notion was growing.

"Eh, I don't know," David said.

"Don't you want to know what happened out there?" she inquired.

"Yeah, sure. I've heard about it since I was a little kid. All of the younger people wonder why older folks don't want to talk about it."

"My dad and stepmom think the place was a thieves camp, not a colony."

"See, that's exactly what they want us to think," he bemoaned. "Everyone says so."

"But how do you know that's a made up story?" she asked.

"I don't know the exact source of the info, but some say there was a survivor from the colony still alive somewhere, maybe even two," he said.

"But you said they were killed."

"They were, but it's believed that some of them might have gotten away. No one knows where."

"What else do you know about the colony?" she questioned.

"That's it. I don't know much. I've told you all that I've heard," he insisted.

Lee Ann's thoughtful eyes searched his face.

"Well let's go see what we can find," she said, turning to grab her army-green jacket from a hook by the door. David watched her every move.

"Do you usually stare like that?" she asked.

"Oh, sorry," he said, becoming self-conscious.

Lee Ann turned to exit the back door as David got out of his chair and took his plate to the sink, running water over it. She turned and smiled for a second, realizing how happy she was to have David's company at that moment. If he had not come over, she knew that she would have been alone with memories she wanted to shut out, regardless of how she treasured them.

The day was overcast with intermittent breezes that chilled the bones. Dark gray clouds blotted the sun and cast a pall over the swaying branches of the forest. Lee Ann pushed aside any feelings of foreboding that such a day might produce, wanting to appear brave in front of David. Immediately, she began to move through the woods, not even pausing to see if David was keeping up. He closed the gap between them in seconds, falling in right behind her.

"Trying to lose me?" he joked.

"Try and keep up," she teased. They crossed the small stream and went on through the larger hardwoods that bordered the reserve. Soon, the small sign that signaled the border of the reserve came into view.

"Wow, you do live close to the reserve," he realized.

"Yep. Ordinarily, I would be thrilled about that," she responded, pausing to look at the sign.

They began their walk down into the hollow then up the rocky hillside, the same way that Lee Ann had gone the first time. Once at the top of the hill, they both stopped to take in the view of the seemingly endless forest that cloaked the hillsides.

"It's not Widow's Bluff, but that's quite the view," David said.

"Yea," she agreed. They went on to cross the dry streambed and into the hollow where Lee Ann had turned around before. Again, she stopped, listening to the sounds around her and surveying her surroundings. In the daylight, she noticed the diversity of the trees in the hollow, admiring the beeches and tulip trees that did not reside among the oaks and hickories of the hilltops. It did not seem to be the same place, although Lee Ann was quite sure that it was.

"What is it?" he asked.

"This is where I was when the voice became fully formed, asking for help," she said.

"Yep. That is what others have claimed to hear. No one I know, but others," he added.

"So, you don't think I'm crazy or anything?"

"No, of course not. There's something that happened here. I believe in hauntings and such—like the old Gray's cemetery outside of town. It's totally haunted," he shared.

"Well, right now we're in Thief's Hollow," she reminded him.

"No, it's a little ways on. I studied the map before I came. It's beyond the next hill," he confidently stated.

"Oh," Lee Ann said, feeling silly about getting too scared before she even reached the site of the colony. The hill that climbed from the empty stream bed was even steeper than the last, and with more rocks. A cave bluff appeared to their right as they neared the crest.

"That'd be a good place to look for arrowheads," David pointed out.

"Maybe later. I want to see this colony, or what's left of it, in the daylight," she said.

Once they reached the top of the hill, Lee Ann was mildly disappointed to find that it did not afford the view the last hill had. Instead, there was more growth on this hill, indicating a difference in age from this part of the forest to the rest. It seemed to Lee Ann that a fire had claimed part of the forest long ago, stopping at the top of the hill. The slope on the other side was gentler and less severe than the last. Through the obscured view, Lee Ann spied something that seemed to be a pile of stone.

"Do you see that?" she said, pointing down into the hollow.

"That's the place, or what's left of it," he said.

They hurried down the gradual slope to the bottom. Here, the forest regained its old growth characteristics as ancient tulip trees rose up to meet them. They crossed a small stream, a bit larger than the one on Lee Ann's property. Somehow, the gurgle of the stream, which should have been a comforting sound, seemed to be swallowed up into the lonely vacuum of the forest. It was then that Lee Ann's eyes shifted to the right, finding the pile of rock she'd spied from the summit.

It looked to be all that remained of a chimney. To the right of this was a mostly smooth, stone foundation, with occasional fissures where decaying weeds had begun to grow. Catty-corner to the remains of the building was a collapsed barn. The rotting timbers had collapsed in on themselves, making it resemble a blackened woodpile more than the remains of a structure.

"Wow, this is it!" David said, pleased with their finding.

Lee Ann, however, wasn't pleased. She'd become filled with emotions that could best be described as fear and panic. The sounds of the distressed voice echoed in her memory, along with flashes of the child's face and the bleeding woman's glassed-over eyes. Lee Ann shook her head, as if she could free herself of the feeling with this gesture. The resemblance to the images she'd seen in her dream were too much for her.

"You okay?" David asked, grabbing her arm gently.

Lee Ann took a deep breath, looking more closely at the remains of the barn. It was apparent when she looked again that the wood was scorched black as if it had been burned.

"No, I have to leave this place. NOW!" she said, turning to run up the rise. The increasing sense of trepidation was more than she could bear, although she didn't understand why. A cloud of dread seemed to surround her, filling her with panic like the remembrance of a traumatic, life-threatening event.

"Wait!" he said, pausing to take a few quick shots of the remains of the buildings with his cell phone. The picture captured the cracked foundation and the rotting timbers, which looked like an abandoned woodpile. He caught up with her at the top, still trying to talk to her.

However, she kept on running over the next two hills and didn't answer him until she'd safely crossed back over onto her own land, some three miles away. He caught his breath after stopping beside Lee Ann at the spring creek.

"What happened back there? You see somethin'?" he asked.

"Not exactly. It was more like a feeling. I don't want to try and remember it all right now. Suffice it to say, it was terrible. Something truly awful and traumatic happened there." She took a deep breath to try and calm herself."I feel as if I have a connection to that place, and I need to know what it is."

CHAPTER 7
THAT WHICH IS LOST WILL RETURN

Lee Ann was anxious to get back to school once her suspension was over. Ever since her experience with David, she was unable to think about anything else besides the mystery surrounding Thief's Hollow. The past two nights she stayed up as late as she could stand, fearing the dreams she might have and what horrors they might show. She lay restless in her bed, and in her anxiety, she turned toward her memories of her mother and what she might have said about the situation.

If only she were here, I know she would know what to do. She would have some insight into what this all means.

Her thoughts traveled back to events a little over a year before when her first boyfriend, Steve, broke up with her. Lee Ann recalled how devastating it had felt, laughing at herself for believing then that her break-up would bring about the end of her world. Her mother had sat down on the bed beside her, pulled her bangs out of her face so that she could see her eyes and put her arm around her. Lee Ann's glassy, mournful eyes stared into her mother's.

"Honey, I know you're hurting right now and how it seems like nothing will make the pain go away. Let me reassure you that it will pass, as hard as it is to see right now. Think of Steve as a rehearsal for when the right one comes along. Even though he might have felt like "the One", he is only the first. A girl with as much going for herself as you have will have no problem finding someone else further down the line. You have your whole life ahead of you, even though it feels like this is some sort of ending. My mother used to tell me that we never lose things in life because what feels like a loss in the present gains us something in the future. What is lost transforms and returns later in a form even more beautiful and right for us than what came before." The certainty with which her mother had delivered those words, along with her reassuring smile, made Lee Ann instantly feel better. She had even laughed slightly, feeling a bit silly for thinking that her loss would consume her.

Coming back to the present, Lee Ann could almost smell the perfume her mother used to wear and feel her mother's arm around her. The idea of this comfort allowed her to fall into a deep sleep, free from dreams of the nearby hollow, and to awake feeling somewhat refreshed.

In the morning, Lee Ann felt a sense of determination and newfound bravery. She put on her favorite black leggings and plaid skirt and slid a white Siouxsie and the Banshees t-shirt over her head, ready to face her fellow students again. As she walked into the building, she swore that almost everyone cast a glance her way. Katrina ran up to her before she could even reach her locker. So far, Mary and her crew were nowhere to be seen.

"I'm so glad you're back! It has been monumentally boring without you here," Katrina said with a smile. Lee Ann smiled back as they made their way to Lee Ann's locker.

"Any more trouble from of our favorite bullies?" Lee Ann asked as she got out her math book.

"Nothing more than dirty looks. Mother tells me that bullies are like angry gorillas. It's best not to establish eye contact with them," Katrina responded, prompting a laugh from Lee Ann. David appeared behind them a second later, making Katrina jump.

"Ugh, stop doing that! Why do you always have to sneak up?" Katrina snapped.

"Sorry, I don't mean to," David answered as he ran his hands through his hair, moving it out of his eyes. Lee Ann turned around and smiled at him; he smiled back. They stared at one another as if Katrina wasn't even present. David made no effort to greet Katrina, causing her to roll her eyes. To her it seemed that David and Lee Ann were in their own world, which didn't include her. She grumbled and walked off.

"Wait, where are you going?" Lee Ann asked.

"Where I don't feel like a third wheel," she answered.

"Oh, sorry," Lee Ann said as her eyes moved from David to Katrina. "Don't go."

Katrina paused a moment, then rejoined her friend at the lockers.

"So what's up with this legend in the woods? Did you find anything else out about it?" Katrina asked.

"Nothing more than bad feelings," Lee Ann recalled.

"What do you mean?" Katrina probed as her eyes moved back and forth between Lee Ann and David.

"Well, Lee Ann and I went to the hollow to check out the site of the colony . . ." David shared.

"You did that without me? No fair!" Katrina protested.

"It was during school," Lee Ann responded, knowing that Katrina would likely never skip school for any reason.

"So? I would have come if an invitation had been extended," Katrina said, sounding hurt.

"It wasn't a plan of any kind. David just showed up unannounced," Lee Ann explained.

"Oh, I see." Katrina softened her tone and took a breath. "Well, did you find anything?"

"Only the foundation of an old house and a pile of burned wood," David stated matter-of-factly.

"And I experienced the creepiest sensation," Lee Ann added.

"Oh yeah? Do tell," Katrina moved in closer, holding her books tightly against her chest.

"I don't know exactly—it was just a sense that something terrible had happened there. I could feel panic and some sort of evil presence."

Katrina's eyes grew wide as she swallowed hard. "So what did you do?"

"Got the hell out of there," Lee Ann responded.

"Did you see anything?" Katrina asked, looking back and forth at them again.

"No," David said, as if he didn't think there was anything to be alarmed about.

"Well, you better tell me the next time you decide to go," Katrina insisted.

"Alright then, I have an idea. This time you are totally invited," David reassured Katrina.

"Ok, let's hear it, Einstein," Katrina teased.

"Why don't we go out there and camp overnight? Then, if we hear or see anything we can try and capture it." David was glowing, grinning from ear to ear at the cleverness of his suggestion.

Lee Ann and Katrina exchanged uncomfortable glances.

"Come on, it will be fun!" David declared.

"I feel like I've seen this movie before," Katrina stated skeptically.

"I don't know. Besides, my dad will never let me camp out with you guys without an adult present. Especially if there's a boy there," Lee Ann said.

David shook his head and laughed.

"Haven't you ever lied to your parents to do something they told you not to?"

Lee Ann was about to answer when she realized that she never had lied to either her mother or father. She did not want to look like a square in front of David but deep down she was proud of her honesty.

"I . . ." Lee Ann hesitated.

"You haven't, I can tell," David teased.

Katrina stepped in to protect her friend. "So what if she hasn't? Not everyone is out to pull the wool over their parent's eyes so they can get away with some form of delinquency."

David rolled his eyes, annoyed at how Katrina always found a way to sneak in larger than normal vocabulary words.

"I suppose I could tell them that I'm going for a sleepover at Katrina's," Lee Ann said, ignoring Katrina's defense.

Katrina's mouth fell open. "So, you're going to go along with his idea?"

"So are you, come on," Lee Ann encouraged, giving her a soft punch on her shoulder. Katrina sighed and flared her nostrils.

"Oh, alright. I suppose I can tell my parents I'm going to spend the night at your house," Katrina said, allowing her curiosity to win.

"That's the spirit!" David exclaimed.

"Could you use some other word?" Lee Ann asked. Before he could answer, Mary, Lisa, and Jenn came walking down the hallway and stopped behind David. Lee Ann clenched her jaw and frowned, bracing herself for another confrontation.

"Well, look who's back?" Mary taunted. David whirled around to confront them.

"Mary, leave her alone," he insisted.

"David, what's gotten into you? If I remember correctly, you used to be cool. I haven't forgotten that time in your truck," Mary said, lifting her left eyebrow. Lee Ann's eyes widened as she searched David's face to see if what Mary said was true.

"That was one time and we both agreed it was a mistake, remember?" David said. Lisa and Jenn whispered to each other and looked Lee Ann's way, contemptuously.

"Well, be careful not to make any other, um, mistakes by hooking up with some freak girl from Nashville," Mary added, before continuing down the hall.

"So, what happened in your truck?" Lee Ann questioned.

"Nothing much. We just kind of made out a bit. It was just a kiss," David recounted.

"Why would you want to kiss that blonde banshee?" Katrina asked.

"I don't know. It was last year. It didn't mean anything," he insisted. "It was at a bonfire party and I had been drinking."

Lee Ann felt like a square again. She had only been drunk once when her friend Hanna's parents were out of town. They had put a small amount of liquor from three bottles into a plastic cup and passed it back and forth. It tasted awful but made them giggle as they talked deep into the night. She imagined David had probably had alcohol several times.

"Come on, Lee Ann, we're going to be late for Science," Katrina announced, as if she couldn't stand to be in the presence of anyone who'd kissed Mary Hartford.

"Coming," Lee Ann said, not bothering to acknowledge David.

"I'll see you later, right?" David asked, seeking reassurance.

"Yep," Lee Ann answered, still not sure what to think about what she had just heard.

"We're going out there!" David shouted at them down the hall as they began to walk away. They feigned not to hear him and didn't answer.

On her way out the door at the end of the day, Lee Ann saw David waiting for her. His friends, who had been talking with him, left as soon as they saw her coming.

"I don't want you to think that I have any feelings for Mary," David declared as soon as his friends were out of earshot.

"Why should I care?" Lee Ann was trying to appear disinterested.

"I don't know. I just . . .well . . ."

Lee Ann laughed at seeing him so nervous. That was one of the things that she liked most about David: the way he went from a cool exterior to vulnerable in a matter of seconds.

"What's funny?" he asked.

"You," Lee Ann laughed.

"So, are we going out there sometime soon?" he inquired as he shuffled his feet nervously.

"Sure, maybe whatever is out there will reveal some secret to us. Though I'm pretty sure it's not going to be pleasant. There's an evil presence there."

"Don't worry, I'll be there with you," he said, putting his hands on her shoulders. Although she knew deep down that the idea of him being able to shield her from some supernatural presence was ridiculous, it still comforted her.

That night, Lee Ann sat in bed, thinking about David's idea. When her eyelids finally became heavy and she began to nod off, a distant sound caused her to jerk suddenly awake . She threw the covers from her legs and ran to the window, peering into the obscured darkness of the woods beyond the garden. There was nothing but the dim moonlight that shone through thin clouds.

Turning back toward the bed, Lee Ann yawned. Then, she heard the sound again; it was the unmistakable female voice she'd heard before. This time, it seemed clearer, more human in origin, although it was too distant for her to make out the words. Immediately, she sat down on the bed and pulled on her boots. She took her black peacoat off the hook by the door and threw it on over the black, short-sleeved shirt and red pajama bottoms she wore.

Once in the yard, she shivered at the sudden intrusion of the cold air in her face. The stillness and silence of the night were enough to make Lee Ann's teeth chatter. Nonetheless, she made her way toward the edge of the woods, straining to hear whatever sounds might issue from there.

She did not have long to wait before the voice called out again. This time, she swore she heard another distinct voice coming from even further away, different in tone from the other. At the same time, she could feel an odd tingling sensation in her hands, as if they'd gone to sleep.

"Help! Please help!" the closer voice spoke. This time there was no hesitation, as if the disembodied presence had learned to form its words more clearly.

"I'm here. How can I help you?" Lee Ann asked, feeling a mixture of fear and fascination as she stepped into the woods, a few yards from the creek she loved so dearly.

"I don't know where to go," the voice returned. "Please help. They're going to get me if I don't get out of here!"

"Who is going to get you?" Lee Ann questioned, scrunching up her eyes to make out whatever she could see as the clouds obscured the bright moon. By now, she should have heard the sound of someone's footsteps crunching the leaves of the forest floor, but no such sound could be heard.

As Lee Ann crossed the stream her eyes caught something, which at first she thought was the reflection of moonlight on the surface of the spring creek. However, the moon continued to be shrouded by clouds. The light was emanating from a bluish orb that hovered close to eye level. Rubbing her eyes, Lee Ann tried to make sure her eyes weren't deceiving her, but the orb was still there, moving slowly toward her.

She took a step backward and swallowed hard as her eyes focused on a slight, transparent figure beginning to materialize around the orb. It was the face of a caucasian woman with her hair tied back. The expression on the woman's face was full of fear and confusion. The clouds moved past the moon, creating a stark contrast between the moon's warm glare and the dark silhouettes of the trees.

"They are coming!" the woman said in a clear voice that echoed, as if it had issued from a deep grotto.

Lee Ann took another step back, not knowing what to say or do, wrapping her arms around herself to stave off her shivers.

She could hear the other female voice, closer than before. This time, there was a sound coming from further in the distance that she hadn't heard. It sounded like barking dogs mixed with male voices.

Flight response took over as Lee Ann turned around and broke into a full run toward the house.

"Wait!" The female voice called out but Lee Ann did not respond or stop her retreat toward the house.

Do not fear, Lee Ann. The comforting voice that Lee Ann had heard in her dream reassured her. She wanted to ask it questions but she was breathing too hard, focused on getting away. Once she got inside, she locked the door and caught her breath, staring out into the night, expecting the figure to emerge from the woods but nothing stirred.

After a few moments, she made her way back into bed. She sat shivering with the covers pulled up to her chin for what seemed like several hours, staring out the window. The only thing that was visible was the comforting moon that had moved away completely from the veil of clouds.

Finally, Lee Ann's exhausted and fearful mind drifted into an uneasy sleep, from which she soon awoke, turning her attention back toward the window. The night still seemed as black and opaque as ever due to the absence of the moonlight that had tempered the darkness earlier. Lee Ann got out of bed and walked slowly to the window, not expecting to see anything.

Much to her surprise, the figure of the woman was hiding behind the storage shed, only a few yards from the back door, peering up at her with a desperate look in her eyes.

Although the figure was still transparent, Lee Ann could make out her features and clothes clearly. She could now tell the woman was middle-aged from the care-worn lines around her eyes.

Another orb was emerging from the woods, followed by others that seemed to be moving rather quickly, as if chasing the closer orb. Lee Ann pulled back from the window instinctively but did not look away.

Once she reached the wall, she sank to the floor, clutching her knees tightly. She was unable to stop herself from shivering or grinding her teeth, despite the heat that emitted from the vent above her head. Although she could no longer see any of the figures, she was still staring at the window too afraid to look away or go to sleep.

CHAPTER 8
TO GUIDE YOU ON YOUR WAY

The next morning, the dark circles under Lee Ann's eyes revealed the lack of sleep she got after the night's events. To Lee Ann, it was apparent that whatever was happening was beginning to increase in its intensity. She feared something deeper than the voices, orbs, or even the desperation of the transparent figure reaching out to her for some sort of help. What concerned her most was the fear that these phenomena would intensify to a fever pitch, that she would be propelled deeply into a world beyond, from which there might be no escape back into the reality of the present. The origin of this feeling was intuitive but also supported by the encounters she'd had.

The creaking of the bedroom door jolted Lee Ann from her trance of staring out the window, covers pulled up to her neck.

"Lee Ann, you alright?" Charles asked, slightly alarmed at his daughter's appearance.

Nodding her head, Lee Ann tried to manage a smile for her father, not wanting to share any more of what she'd experienced than she had to. She felt that full disclosure would only increase the likelihood that Shirley would try to convince her father that she needed some help.

"Just bad dreams. I'm okay," she reassured him. Charles knew his daughter well enough to know when she was trying to deflect.

"You don't seem alright. Lately, it's as if you're in some sort of trance. You also look like you haven't slept. Please let me know what I can do to help you. Don't shut me out," he implored, taking her cold hand in his own.

Her eyes locked with her father's and she smiled again, thinking of how she wanted to open up to him and tell him everything the way she would have with her mother, but she was unsure of what the outcome would be. In the past, her mother was always open to her perspective and would always listen to her daughter's concerns carefully.

"I think it's all just part of the grieving process," she offered. This, at least, was a partial truth.

"Maybe we need to get you some counseling. Talkin' to a professional might make you feel better," he suggested as he squeezed her hand. The warmth of his grip and his intentions offered some small comfort. However, she knew that listening to someone tell her everything was some figment of her imagination, a byproduct of her grief, wouldn't help even if it were true. From what she had heard and read about therapists, she didn't have much faith in their methods.

"I think I just need some time is all. It heals all wounds, right?" she said, feeling slightly embarrassed to be embracing a cliché that her father had used just a short time ago.

"I hope so, but I want you to know that you can always talk to me about what's going on with you," he offered.

This gave her some comfort but also made her feel guilty at the way she had characterized her old man. Before she came to live with him, she always thought that her time on the weekends with him was something that she just had to endure. She had thought of him as a rural simpleton, despite his abilities to fix just about any hunk of junk and work with his hands. The way that he was able to listen to the rumble of an engine and immediately come up with an accurate diagnosis was not lost on her. She felt that she possessed very little of this innate ability.

Like her mother, she had what she felt were less practical abilities: a strong, intuition coupled with artistic talent. There was a wisdom and kindness in Charles' eyes that Lee Ann knew she hadn't given him credit for. Perhaps it was the slight resentment she still felt toward him for breaking up the family so long ago; for putting his own needs above his family's.

Now, she felt like she had a window into what her mother must have seen in him so long ago.

"Thanks, Dad. I'll remember that," she said.

He sat there a moment longer as if hoping that she would reveal more to him, but soon he got up and left her alone.

It was Saturday and the sun had banished the clouds of the previous evening. Lee Ann took a deep breath, knowing that she had to be strong and not allow whatever was happening to overwhelm her. She decided to do some digging into the legend. Online searches had turned up very little, just a few discussions in some chat rooms concerning the paranormal. The only thing she had managed to uncover in this regard was a thread on one of the sites, which featured a debate between those who believed the 'thief' account and those that felt there was a cover up of something sinister.

Her plan was to go into town to see what she could discover in the local library. The idea that she would need to resort to such a tactic in the age of the internet was funny to her, but this was about something that occurred a long time ago in a small town. Furthermore, the conflicting accounts aroused suspicion for Lee Ann.

After a quick shower, Lee Ann put on a v-neck sweater her mother had given her along with tights and a skirt. Shirley and Charles went silent when she appeared in the kitchen.

"Well, look who decided to join the land of the living," Shirley said. The statement left Lee Ann feeling uneasy, although she knew Shirley didn't mean it the way it sounded.

"I'm feeling much better, thanks," Lee Ann said, managing to smile.

"I was thinking we might do some fishing or something this weekend. What do you say?" Charles queried.

"Maybe tomorrow. I actually have a school project that I need to do some research for," she revealed.

"Well, I hope you can get a strong enough signal to do the research you need," Charles said.

"Actually, this project involves local history. I'm going to go visit the library," Lee Ann stated. Shirley creased her forehead, not expecting a teenager to seek answers to anything in a place other than the internet.

"The library? Didn't know that people went there anymore," Shirley chimed in.

"Sure they do," Charles offered in his daughter's defense. "Especially if you are lookin' for something involving local history. I think it's great that you're going to find out more about the place you're from. All this time I felt like you were ashamed to be from Pearson County; ashamed to be from such a small place in the country."

"Of course not," Lee Ann said, knowing full well that she wasn't being completely honest.

"What period of local history are you looking into?" Shirley asked. Lee Ann was hoping to avoid specifics, but she knew that her parents were both thinking of Thief's Hollow.

"Not sure yet. We are supposed to pick something that happened in the area and write an informative essay on it," she said. Now she was telling an outright lie, which she wasn't proud of, but she felt this was a necessary evil in order to avoid having to listen to their reassurances about the legend.

Shirley and Charles exchanged a look. Charles was trying to communicate to his wife that she shouldn't pursue this line of questioning. As if sensing this, she backed down and didn't ask any further questions.

"If you'd still like to go fishing, try and be back by three so we can get to a good spot for the afternoon," he said.

"Ok, will do," she said, grabbing a cold piece of toast from a plate on the kitchen table beside her.

As she began the long walk into town, she took out her phone and thought about texting David and Katrina, but something told her this might only be a distraction when some intensive research was needed, so she refrained from it. It was a three mile walk, but her mounting curiosity about the story of the colony drove her on. She did notice that David had sent her something on Instagram: it was a picture he had taken of her and Katrina the first week that she'd attended school. Although only a few weeks had gone by, it seemed like she had known her friends much longer. They were standing by the lockers smiling. Although she liked the picture, she did not comment.

As time passed, Lee Ann knew that David was growing more and more fond of her, but she still didn't quite know how she felt. She was consumed by her grief, the women in the woods, and the evil presence they escaped from. Without these things to contend with, she knew she'd likely be spending more time with him.

Lee Ann continued on her way to the town library. The deep woods lining the road gave way to occasional houses and buildings; she looked at the burned out automobiles and the trailers with assorted junk in the yards and began to see things differently than she had before.

Yes, many of these people were probably less sophisticated than some that she had known in Nashville, they may have held beliefs that were less than broad-minded, and clung to traditions and norms she might not understand, but she wondered what hidden talents and skills they might possess, and what stories many of them could tell. Lee Ann heard a truck with several young men come up behind her, slowing down as it approached.

"Need a ride?" a boy in a cowboy hat asked her as they stopped beside her. Lee Ann turned towards him.

"No thanks, I like walking," she said.

"Suit yourself, babe," he replied as the others stared at her. The truck sped off into town. Although she didn't particularly like being called 'babe' or the way they were looking at her, she decided to keep quiet just to avoid confrontation.

The library was located on a side street off of Main Street where Lee Ann walked past a pet store, a gun shop, The Winston Hotel, and several other local businesses. A solitary car drove past as a few pedestrians walked down the sidewalk. She got a few off-kilter looks, but most of the people were friendly. This veneer of small town southern friendliness was something that she was beginning to welcome. She thought about sitting on one of the benches, getting out her sketchpad, and drawing her surroundings—something she normally reserved for the woods. Instead, she turned and went down Johnston Street until she found the small, nondescript, concrete building that was the town library.

An elderly woman with thin, pointed reading glasses looked up from the circulation desk as soon as she entered. It seemed obvious that the woman was surprised to see a young person there.

"Hello, dear. Is there anything I can help you find today? One of our computers is unoccupied if you need it," she said with a slow twang.

"Actually, I was interested in the local section," Lee Ann revealed. The woman's eyebrows rose, causing her spectacles to fall lower on the bridge of her nose.

"Really? What are you trying to find out, if you don't mind me asking?"

Lee Ann surveyed the building to see who might overhear her inquiry. Her eyes landed on a middle-aged woman who was sitting at one of four tables toward the back, reading a paper. Her face was obscured by long, silver and white locks of hair. She was dressed in a dark floral print dress that reminded Lee Ann of the dresses her mother used to wear.

"I'm interested in local legends," Lee Ann stated.

"Oh really? Well, the local section is in a small room on the back left next to the restroom," she answered. Lee Ann nodded and hurried in that direction to avoid any more questioning.

Once inside the room, Lee Ann was struck by what appeared to be something out of another era. There were old stacks of newspapers preserved in plastic on one wall, a glass case filled with city memorabilia in the dead center of the room, and a few microfiche machines lining the opposite wall. She had no idea how to even use such archaic machines. A sign next to the machines read: 'Newspapers older than the year 2000 are preserved on film in the case next to the microfiche readers.' Lee Ann's eyes shifted to the case. She knew that she needed to be looking at the mid-forties, but had no idea what year or month. Either out of curiosity, or perhaps as a means of surveillance, the librarian entered the room.

"Did you need any help?" she asked.

"Actually, I do. I know I need to use the microfiche, but to be honest I have no idea how to," Lee Ann answered, welcoming the woman's presence.

"Why sure, hun. I'm just glad to see someone making use of 'em. It probably won't be long before they remove them," the woman said. This statement saddened Lee Ann, thinking about how somber it was that old memories and events could be removed and stored somewhere where no one could see or recall them, about how this would negate the lives and happenings of people long since passed.

"Do you know which years or months you need? I'm afraid we only have the local paper, *The Laverne Times* after a certain date."

"That's fine. I know I want to see articles from the mid-forties, but to tell the truth I have no idea what year or month exactly," Lee Ann answered. Another look of astonishment passed over the woman's face.

"Forties, eh? Anything in particular?"

"The incident at Thief's Hollow," Lee Ann blurted out. The woman's eyebrows arched up even further.

"Oh, well now that's forty-four. I was only a little girl, but I remember it well. October, I believe it was."

"Wow, what do you remember about it?" Lee Ann was fascinated and wanted to find out as much as she could from the story.

"Well, dear, I remember how proud I felt of the sheriff and his men for saving our community."

"What happened, exactly?"

"Well, as I recall, the adults were talking a lot about robberies that had occurred in nearby places, Hohenwald and Columbia, I believe. Not too long after the talk began, the thieves killed the wife of Gerald Langston, a rich man right here in town. Then, there were some hunters that spied a camp deep in the woods at Thief's Hollow. This was before the State bought up the land and turned it into a wildlife preserve. They even caught a glimpse of some of the men in that camp who fit the description of the thieves that had been placed on wanted posters like they did back in those days. The hunters revealed what they saw to the local authorities. Apparently, there was a shootout in the woods. The thieves would not come quietly. Many of the sheriff's men, as well as some of the local men who agreed to help, were killed. Only the sheriff and one deputy survived. Although the sheriff claimed that all the thieves were killed, some of them may have survived. There were some rumors going around that contradicted the sheriff's account, but most people didn't believe them.

No one is really sure. Either way, we were all very proud of Sheriff Rogers and his men for taking care of the thieves before they had a chance to prey on our community," she said with a smile. Lee Ann smiled back.

"What do you make of the people who say it was a colony or something else besides a hideout for thieves?" Lee Ann asked.

The woman giggled. "Well, there will always be people who like to spin tall tales about things but the proof is right there in the papers. Here I'll show you," she said. The woman took out a dusty box that read, "September/October 1944, *The Laverne Times*," switched on a light and threaded a small reel through the old machine. She proceeded to show Lee Ann how to turn the crank in order to scroll through the pages.

"Here it is," the woman said, feeling satisfied with how quickly she located the story. The headline read, "Shootout at Thief's Hideout, Sheriff Victorious!"

"I'll leave you to it," the woman said as she got up to leave the room.

"Thank you so much," Lee Ann answered.

"Well, you're welcome, sugar."

Lee Ann devoured the article, looking for any clues that might dispel the 'facts' that the article revealed. She learned very little new information about the incident, other than the names of the deputies and men that were known to have died in the shootout. It seems that very little was known about the thieves themselves, other than the murder that was attributed to them and the vague recollections of robberies in Hohenwald and Columbia, just as the librarian had described them. In fact, mostly the article was a praise of the police department, rather than a detailed recollection of facts surrounding the incident.

In the end, Lee Ann felt a sense of disappointment at what she'd found. It left her with more questions than new, factual information. There was nothing more about the incident in the tiny library and nothing more to be found about the supposed robberies in nearby communities.

When Lee Ann left the local newsroom, the grey-haired woman

sitting at the table at the back of the main room looked up at her. Lee Ann locked eyes with the woman, thinking there was something engaging and warm in the woman's glance. The knowing smile and glint in the woman's hazel eyes was comforting to Lee Ann. She could sense a wisdom there that went beyond anything she'd sensed in any of the other locals.

"Hello," the woman said in a voice devoid of a drawl. The woman's words were thin and wispy, as if carried on the wind. Beside her was a stack of books. She held an open newspaper.

"Hi," Lee Ann said. The librarian was busy scanning returned books at the circulation desk and paid little attention to them.

"Local legends are a curious thing, are they not?" The woman stated matter-of-factly. "I couldn't help but overhear," she said, sensing what Lee Ann's response to this might be.

"Yes, they are," Lee Ann said, wondering what else this woman knew. The woman's eyes were a piercing but friendly steel gray.

"My name is Felicity. Who might you be?" the woman asked.

"Lee Ann Daniels," she responded. The woman nodded, as if she already knew this, but just had it confirmed.

"Would you care to come and sit for a minute?" Felicity asked, pulling the chair out from the table.

"Sure, why not?" Lee Ann answered, sensing that the woman's intentions were good. The librarian had gone into the storeroom for something.

"So, I have to ask. Why are you trying to find out about Thief's Hollow?" Her searching eyes tugged at the honesty in Lee Ann.

"I don't know that I believe what I've heard about it," Lee Ann revealed.

"Oh? Neither do I," she said with a friendly smile.

"You don't? Why?"

"I was going to ask you the same question," Felicity replied.

Lee Ann looked around to see if anyone such as the librarian might be over-hearing them and continued when she was satisfied, "Well, for one thing, I've heard that it was some sort of colony and that there were no actual thieves."

"Is that so? I'm surprised that anyone would actually admit such a thing. Most of the people around here are so hush-hush about it."

"So I see," Lee Ann confirmed.

"There's something more, though. Another reason that you are fascinated with it," Felicity said, stating it as a fact, rather than a question.

"How do you know that?" Lee Ann asked, taken aback.

"Well, I suppose over the years I've developed what might be referred to as a sixth sense about things. You know, when you look at something and see more than what is revealed in the literal sense of the image."

Lee Ann was a bit puzzled at this talk, but deep down she had some sense of what Felicity meant.

"You know, I hold this copy of *Light in August* in my hand and on the surface it just seems like an old book, the cover is now a faded red from age and the pages are beginning to yellow. Further examination reveals certain pages folded in, coffee stains on specific pages and a sense of who owned it before."

"I see," Lee Ann said, although she didn't, not fully.

"I sensed something when you walked in that I haven't felt in some time," Felicity went on. This time, her eyes sparkled, almost mischievously.

"What did you sense?"

Felicity looked around, as if she didn't want prying ears to hear. The librarian was still somewhere in the storage room, so she continued.

"You have a glow about you, a light," Felicity said with a smile.

"What do you mean, exactly?"

"Well, when I was about your age . . . I'm going to guess you're seventeen or maybe sixteen."

"Sixteen," Lee Ann responded.

"Yes, well, around the time I was your age, I began to notice some things that seemed peculiar about the world around me. I even sensed that a person was in my presence, but no one else seemed to notice anyone there. What I felt was more like the perception of someone's energy who was invisible to the naked eye."

"Really?" Lee Ann said, completely enthralled as she propped her chin up with her fist and gave Felicity her undivided attention.

"You can perceive such things as well, can you not?"

Lee Ann felt both excited and relieved to have found someone who she could not only share these things with, but someone who could actually relate.

"Well, there were voices, coming from the woods. It was a woman's voice that could not fully form words, at first. Then, the voice was clearly asking for help. Next, the dreams began and I began to see this terrible scene in which these two women were trying to escape. I heard gunfire and finally saw one of the women lying in a pool of blood." Lee Ann had to catch her breath, she was sharing things so excitedly.

Felicity's pupils grew larger and the smile vanished from her face.

"Go on. What happened next?" Felicity probed.

"A friend of mine and I visited the hollow and I was overcome with a terrible sense of tragedy and dread. I don't know what it was but I knew I had to get out of there because there was some kind of malice or evil presence that lingered there. Last night, I heard the voices again—two of them. One was quite close to the edge of the woods behind our house and another from deeper in the woods. Then, I saw her."

"What did you see, exactly?" Felicity put her hand on Lee Ann's arm. It felt warm and reassuring.

"At first it was kind of a colorful but transparent orb. A moment later, I could see the transparent figure of a woman. I could make out her features enough to see that she was middle-aged. She had her hair up and her eyes were confused and scared. She said she didn't know where she was supposed to go but that they were going to get her if she didn't leave."

Felicity looked off into the distance, contemplating everything she'd heard.

"It's as I thought. Something terrible did happen there and it wasn't what we've all been told. You've been given important insight into it," Felicity revealed.

"Why me? I haven't been sleeping and I just want my life to return to normal," Lee Ann said, almost pleadingly.

Felicity took Lee Ann's hand in hers and smiled slightly.

"My dear, I felt exactly the same way at first, but this is not a choice we're given. The hidden world reveals itself to us whether we welcome it or not. Think of it as a gift rather than a curse—a chance to help in some way, if you can."

"But how can I help?"

"Lee Ann, I can't say with any certainty what happened out there, but it could be that there are souls in that place who can't find their way out. They may be trapped in traumatic loops from the tragic events that happened there. You see, sometimes when people leave this plane of existence under dramatic and traumatic circumstances, they cannot free themselves from it, and cannot go on to the next phase of their existence without some help."

"What kind of help?"

"It may be hard to believe, but there are those, both alive and beyond, that can help restless souls make the transition from one plane to the next; spiritual guides of a sort, if you will. To those souls, the presence of such a guide shines out to them like a beacon in the darkness. For they cannot see the way out of the events that have taken their lives on their own."

"But I don't know how to guide them or what to say to them. I only feel fear and pity, and a sense that something more dangerous is out there besides the women I've seen."

"You are right to be cautious, but you must trust in your gifts and believe in your ability to help. All that you need be at this point is open to the possibilities. I can help you," Felicity soothed with a reassuring smile, prompting Lee Ann to smile back.

Lee Ann looked down, suddenly realizing that Felicity wasn't reading a newspaper at all. Inside the paper was a guide to herbs and folk remedies.

"Why are you acting like you're reading the paper?" Lee Ann asked.

"Let's just say that I don't want to attract attention. People already think I'm some kind of witch, so I guess it wouldn't do for me to be caught reading this or they will think I'm trying to cast a spell on someone." Lee Ann and Felicity both laughed.

CHAPTER 9
INVASION

T he following Monday after school, Lee Ann beat a hasty retreat. She began her walk home without stopping to chat with David and Katrina, as she usually did. She wanted to confront her own anxious thoughts, to get past the fears that she felt and see what she could learn from the lost souls near her father's land. Katrina caught sight of her departure and ran up to catch her.

"Wait, Lee Ann, why are you leaving so quickly?" Katrina was anxious to talk with her as she noticed a slight look of worry on Lee Ann's face.

"I have a lot of homework and a lot on my mind," Lee Ann answered abruptly.

David and his group of friends exited the building. David quickly turned his attention away from the group to look for Lee Ann. He saw Lee Ann and Katrina talking by the steps that led away from the building. His friend, Gordon, noticed his diverted attention.

"What is your deal, dude? You've been all over that girl since she came here," Gordon said, adjusting his baseball cap as he reached for a fresh pinch of chewing tobacco, satisfied that no school officials could see them.

"She's cool, man. You should try and get to know people before writin' them off," David said.

"But dude, there are several babes at this school that aren't freaks . . ." Gordon protested.

"I'm starting to rethink the whole definition of what makes someone a freak," David said, before turning to walk away. Gordon looked around again for school officials, shook his head and spat, as if making some sort of commentary with this gesture.

"Hey, what's up?" David said as he came over and stood beside Lee Ann.

"Nothing, I just have a lot of homework and need to get home," she said.

"That's funny, the last time you were about to go home you were scared. What's different?" he asked.

Lee Ann looked around to make sure they were far enough away from any prying ears.

"Well, I've been thinking that the fear I've felt isn't helpful. I mean, these souls or whoever they are, are in need of help. They aren't there to attack me or cause me any harm. I saw a woman who was desperate and afraid . . ."

"What about the thing they're running from? Isn't there a logical reason to fear whatever that might be?" Katrina asked as she leaned in.

"Yes, but if I can help them I have to try," Lee Ann insisted emphatically.

"Why you? How can you help them?" David added. Lee Ann looked around again just to be sure no one overheard.

"I'm not sure what to make of it but I met someone in the library who said they recognized something in me," she explained.

"Who?" David asked.

"A woman. She was middle-aged and had grayish streaks in her hair. She seemed very different from anyone else I've met around these parts," Lee Ann gave a fake southern inflection on the last three words of her statement.

"Was her name Felicity, by any chance?" David asked, shaking his head.

"Yeah, that's it! Do you know her?"

"Eh, no. I know *of* her. People say she's some kind of pagan or witch. No one around here has anything to do with her."

"Sounds like a typical small town reaction to an independent-minded woman. I'll bet there isn't even a reason for people to feel that way," Katrina speculated.

"Well, maybe you're right, but I wouldn't put too much stock in what she has to say. People say she's downright crazy," David said.

"So? Why do you believe that? What reason do you have to think that, other than the rumor mill?" Lee Ann asked, frowning. Katrina nodded her head in agreement.

"Eh, well. I guess I don't have one." David shrugged as his face curved into a slight frown. "Anyway, what did she say?"

"She said that she sensed that I have a gift. She says some souls that become lost need a guide to help them find their way to the next plane. She says that my presence shines out to them like some sort of homing beacon."

"Wow that's cool and also kind of freaky!" David responded, not sure what to make of it all.

"Tell me about it, " Lee Ann remarked.

"So you're hurrying home to see if you can communicate with them again and somehow help them?" Katrina ascertained.

"I guess. I didn't get the chance yesterday because I was fishing with my dad most of the day. The more I think about what Felicity told me, the more I feel curious and hopeful, rather than afraid," Lee Ann concluded.

"Well, that's an improvement I guess," David said.

Just behind David, an African-American girl appeared. She had long, braided hair which she'd dyed red. They were all surprised to see her because there weren't all that many students of color at the school and they kept mostly to themselves.

"Hello," she said in a shy, low voice.

"Hi," Lee Ann said with a smile.

"Sorry to interrupt your conversation but I couldn't help but over-hear," she said as a slight smile moved across her face. Lee Ann's own smile ran away as she realized they had been talking loud enough to attract attention.

"My name's Jasmine, by the way. I've heard you guys talking about Thief's Hollow before. I think I might be able to help you."

Lee Ann, Katrina, and David all looked around at each other. They were both amazed and pleased to hear her words.

"I'm Lee Ann and this is Katrina and David," Lee Ann pointed to each as the smile returned to her face.

Lee Ann extended her hand as a welcoming gesture.

"Nice to meet you," Jasmine gave her another shy smile.

"So how do you think you can help?" Katrina jumped in abruptly.

Jasmine looked around and waved for them to follow her further away from the schoolyard to the edge of the woods. She didn't want the other students to hear them and start floating rumors around the school about what she was going to share.

"My Grandmother Roberta told me about the place they call Thief's Hollow just last year. I'd asked my family about it because I heard some kids at school talking. She told me that the rumors I'd heard weren't true. I asked her what really happened there and she said she couldn't tell me the specifics." She paused to check the area for any prying ears. After seeing no one, she continued. "When I asked why, she told me it was for my own safety and that maybe one day she could tell me. What she did reveal is that she actually lived in that hollow when she was really little."

"She lived there with the thieves?" Katrina asked in disbelief.

"No, that's just it. There weren't any thieves, just people. That's all I know," Jasmine shrugged.

"So what happened to them? Why were they there and where did they go?" Lee Ann asked eagerly, her mind brimming with questions.

"That's all I know, sorry. Grandma wouldn't tell me anything else. She said she just wanted me to know the rumors weren't true and that she would tell me more about it when she was ready. I wish I had more information for you," Jasmine said. She could tell her new friends were as fascinated by the legend as she was, and she had a gut feeling that she could trust them.

The others looked around at each other again, mystified at this latest piece of information.

"So where is your grandmother now?" Lee Ann inquired.

"She lives in Blue Spruce. It's about an hour away. We can't get her to come anywhere near this area, although she's originally from around here. If I want to visit her, I have to go there," Jasmine shared.

"That's really crazy," David remarked.

"Anyway," Jasmine went on, "I'd love to help you guys if I can. I want to know what happened there, too."

"You're one of us, now," Katrina said and extended her arm out toward the others. The group looked at her quizzically; they didn't know what she expected them to do.

"It's a group huddle. Come on," she explained.

Lee Ann smiled and put her hand on Katrina's. David rolled his eyes, but went ahead and put his hand on the other's. Jasmine's shy smile grew bigger as she put her hand on David's.

Lee Ann felt better knowing she had a group of supporters that actually believed what she was experiencing. It made her anticipation of having to face the overgrown garden and the looming shadow of the woods at twilight behind her house easier to bear.

When she got home, she gave her father a perfunctory greeting, choosing not to say anything further about her experiences. Charles asked questions but didn't get much out of his daughter.

"You've been a bit quiet lately, hun. Everything alright? Not hearing or seeing anything strange lately, are you?" His brow creased upward with concern.

"No, nothing new to report, thanks Dad. I have a lot of homework to get to, so I'd better get started," she said, making a hasty retreat for the stairs. He smiled and let her go, not fully believing her.

In her room, Lee Ann distracted herself by reading a Kurt Vonnegut novel, *Cat's Cradle*. She laughed at the deadpan, humanist sense of humor displayed in the book, trying to occupy her mind while she waited for nightfall. For a minute, she lay on her back and laughed at the notion of being able to touch things and have them turn to ice as the invention, ice nine, does in the novel. She fell asleep picturing herself turning everything in her room into ice.

When Charles called for Lee Ann to come for dinner, she didn't answer. He went up to check on her and saw her gently snoozing with the paperback on her chest, rising and falling with her breath.

He put a plate of pizza and a salad on her bedside table and left the room.

Lee Ann snoozed peacefully until the warm glow of the moonlight through the window woke her up. She stretched and noticed the plate by her bed, took a bite of the now-cold pizza and looked out of the window. She expected to see the figure of the helpless woman again at any moment but nothing appeared.

She dropped the slice of pizza back on the plate as she yawned. Struck by a sudden, odd feeling, Lee Ann looked to her arms. The short hairs on her arms were standing up rigidly. Sounds from downstairs caught her attention. She heard footsteps followed by the creak of a door.

At first she thought nothing of this because there were, after all, two other people in the house. She checked the time on the cat clock her mother had given her; its eyes shifted with each swing of its pendulum tail. Although it felt much later, it was only eight thirty. Her curiosity coupled with the strange feelings she was having compelled her to get up and investigate.

At the bottom of the stairs, she had a clear view of the door to her parent's bedroom. The door was slightly ajar and only the bedside lamp was turned on; she peered inside and saw both her father and stepmother lying on the bed watching the television, engaged in their movie.

Lee Ann swallowed nervously. The noise she'd heard hadn't come from her father or Shirley and it seemed her parents had not heard the sound either. They had already proven that they could not see or hear the apparitions as she had, so asking for their assistance would only exacerbate the situation. She decided to check the back kitchen door first to make sure that no one had entered the house that way. A part of her wanted to search the knife drawer for protection against a possible intruder, but deep down she knew that such a weapon was not likely to do her any good.

The door was closed, but what alarmed Lee Ann was the fact that the doorknob was unlocked. Every night, Shirley would lock all of the doors just before she went to bed, despite the fact that many of the people that lived in the surrounding area didn't bother.

The open laundry room door to the right of the kitchen caught Lee Ann's attention. This, too, was unusual because this door stayed closed almost all of the time, unless Shirley was using it. She swallowed and began to quietly walk toward the door. Once she peered inside the room, she was relieved to find it empty, but she slowly walked inside to make certain. As soon as she stepped into the small room, she felt a sensation not unlike static electricity along her arms, making the hairs stand at attention again. She was also struck by the sudden feeling of coldness around her, which she attributed to the window on the far side of the room. Making her way past the washer and dryer, Lee Ann looked through the window out into the garden. Something like a shadow passed before it, moving toward the back door.

I didn't lock the back door, Lee Ann realized with alarm. Taking a deep breath, she tried to think back to what Felicity had told her. If what she was experiencing was indeed restless spirits they were only there because they needed her help. Why should she be fearful? Just as she began to gather her courage, Lee Ann was struck by the feeling of being watched, although she couldn't tell if the presence was behind her or coming from outside.

Slowly, she began to back away, afraid to take her eyes away from where the shadow had passed. Suddenly, she became overwhelmed by the urge to turn around, as the feeling that she was not alone grew.

Whirling around, she immediately felt the presence of some foreign energy that slowly materialized into the familiar silhouette of the woman in the nightgown with the forlorn eyes. The figure was no longer transparent but seemed to display a bluish, otherworldly translucence. Now, Lee Ann could clearly see the woman's features. The woman's eyes were huge and round, as if they had just seen something truly horrific. The wrinkles on her face and hands revealed that she was not a young woman. Lee Ann brought her cold hand up to her mouth and began to back away from the figure, who took a step toward her. Despite the fact that she didn't want to be afraid, shivers surged through her body. She rubbed her hands on her arms to soothe herself.

"Please . . ." The woman said in a voice that had a strange, otherworldly quality to it.

Unable to hold back her fearful urges, Lee Ann let out a shriek, turning away from the woman as she covered her mouth. Staring at her from the edge of the woods was a white man in overalls with the same translucent, glowing appearance. She shrieked again, turning around to find that the woman was now gone. Lee Ann fled from the laundry room and made for the stairs just as her father sat up in bed.

"What the?" he questioned as Shirley awoke, mid-snore, having fallen asleep during the movie.

"What's happening?" she asked. Charles didn't answer. He got out the shotgun in the lower drawer of his bedside table and loaded it with a shell. Slowly, he pushed the door open, motioning with his hand for Shirley to stay in the bed. Making his way into the darkness of the downstairs hallway, he walked with the gun out in front of him past the laundry room and into the kitchen. He saw no evidence of anyone there and lowered the gun.

Hurriedly, he made his way up the stairs and pushed Lee Ann's bedroom door the rest of the way open. He found his daughter sitting up in bed, still shivering from her encounter.

"Are you alright, Lee? I heard a scream downstairs."

Lee Ann quickly struggled to offer an explanation, reluctant to recount the actual events she'd experienced.

"I went downstairs for awhile and fell asleep on the couch. I had a bad dream and woke myself up. Then, I came and got in bed. Sorry to scare you like that," she said, trying to stop herself from shaking. Charles put the gun down on Lee Ann's dresser, next to her mirror where her artifacts dedicated to her mother's memory were displayed, and he took Lee Ann's hand in his. It was unusually cold to the touch.

"Are you sure that's all?" he whispered.

"Yes, Dad. I'm alright now," she reassured him.

"Baby, maybe we need to get you some help—you know, someone to talk to about all of this," he said, squeezing her hand.

"No, it will pass, Dad. I'm sure of it. It's like you said; it's just my way of dealing with the grief. Besides, how can we afford such a thing?"

"We can find a way, if it would help," he said as they exchanged smiles.

Meanwhile, Shirley had put on her nightgown and began to walk nervously around the downstairs area. As she passed the backdoor, she noticed that it was unlocked. Scrunching up her face, she put the chain where it belonged and looked around her cautiously. Not wanting to be alone and feeling unnerved, she made her way for the stairs. Shirley entered Lee Ann's bedroom and looked down at her husband and step-daughter.

"You alright?" she asked. Lee Ann nodded her head as Charles turned to face his wife.

"More bad dreams," he explained.

"Lee Ann, did you unlock the door?" Shirley inquired.

Lee Ann hesitated for a second, not wanting her stepmother to be alarmed by this.

"Before I fell asleep on the couch, I sat on the back porch for a bit. I guess I forgot to lock it. Sorry," she said and tried to reassure her with a smile.

CHAPTER 10

THE BARRIER

Although she wanted to hide it, Lee Ann was now feeling quite alarmed over the role that Felicity wanted her to play. There was only one thing to do: seek the advice of the one person in Pearson County that could help her. She took out the card that Felicity had given her and read it for the first time: *Felicity Taylor, Psychic and Tarot Reader.* There was a crystal ball above the wording. Lee Ann shook her head and for a second she questioned the authenticity of the mysterious woman she befriended at the library.

What if she's a phony? Probably most of the people that offer psychic services are fakes.

In the end, Lee Ann searched her feelings and struggled with her doubt. There was only one way to determine if Felicity was the genuine article. At this point, Lee Ann was desperate for advice. If she didn't do something, these spirits would continue to invade her space and she wouldn't be able to hide the situation from her parents for much longer.

Lee Ann was aware that Charles and Shirley's anniversary was tonight and that they'd be going out for dinner. It seemed like the perfect opportunity for Felicity to come over and assess the situation.

"I knew I'd be hearing from you soon," Felicity announced as soon as she answered the phone.

"Well, you're psychic right, so you would know," Lee Ann responded.

"That's not exactly what I meant. I just knew that you would need some help. They are continuing to try and make contact, aren't they?"

"Yes, they actually came inside the house. I went downstairs and the woman I've been seeing in the woods came into the laundry room. She was trying to communicate but I became frightened and left before I could hear what she had to say. I also saw a man through the window. I wonder just how many of them are out there."

"It's much easier to say this than put into practice but you needn't be afraid of them. They may be in need of guidance and probably do not wish to harm you," Felicity stated in a calm, measured voice.

"Can you help me? My parents are going out for the evening so maybe you can come over and help me help them or something . . ."

"I would rather have your parent's permission but I'm going to go out on a limb and bet they don't know about these restless spirits invading their laundry room," Felicity responded calmly.

"No, they don't. When this all first began to happen, I told dad about the voices and dreams I was having. He told me it might be a symptom of my grief."

"Yes, I can sense the grief but what's happening is not a symptom of it. You've lost the most important person in your life. Yes, your mother. Poor dear, I am so sorry," Felicity consoled.

"It's okay," Lee Ann responded solemnly.

"She is watching over you. I can sense that she wants you to be at peace."

"Can you help me communicate with her?"

"You don't need my help. You already have the ability," Felicity stated with continued calm and reassurance.

Lee Ann thought about the vision in which she sat with her mother in the space above the Earth. Or was it a dream after all?

"For now, let's keep our focus on the matter at hand. What time will your parents be going out?" Felicity pressed.

"They are going to dinner at seven. So can you be here at eight?" Lee Ann asked.

"Yes."

"Thank you so much. It's 2810 Green Creek Road. There's a gravel road and a brown mailbox with the address on it," Lee Ann shared.

"I'll be there."

"You sure you're going to be alright if we go out?" Charles inquired as he straightened his tie in the mirror. It was strange for Lee Ann to see her father in something besides jeans or a hoodie. His tie was too short in the front, revealing the skinnier part in the back and his shirt, a bit too tight. She couldn't help but let out a snicker.

"What's funny?"

"Here, dad," Lee Ann said, adjusting his tie.

"Where would I be without you?"

"To answer your question, I'll be fine."

"Well, I know you've been going through a lot lately and I want you to know you can talk to me about anything. I know how much you miss your mom," Charles offered, thinking about how Lee Ann had begun to resemble a younger version of her mother.

Lee Ann smiled and hugged him, knowing full well that she couldn't talk to him about what had been happening lately. It would only result in them trying to get her professional help, which she knew wouldn't do her or the restless inhabitants of the nearby woods any good.

"That's good to know, dad," she answered, realizing that Shirley was standing in the doorway watching her.

"Charles, let's go," Shirley said, curtly. Her face was rigid and lacking in emotion, and Lee Ann knew she was feeling jealous of her relationship with her father. Although she couldn't confide everything in him, she was beginning to appreciate who he was more than she had when she was just visiting for the weekend.

"We'll be back around nine thirty or so," he said as he walked down the hallway.

"Ok, don't feel like you have to hurry back. I'm fine, I swear," Lee Ann insisted.

Darkness was beginning to fall as the red pick up truck disappeared around a bend in the gravel drive. Lee Ann went downstairs and sat on the porch, awaiting Felicity's arrival. An owl gave out a solitary hoot from somewhere in the large trees behind the house. At eight o'clock on the dot, Felicity drove up in her rusty blue Honda Civic that looked like it might break down any minute.

"Have I missed anything?" Felicity asked as she got out of the car. She was wearing another floral print dress with a brown cardigan.

"Nothing yet," Lee Ann answered from the porch.

As soon as Felicity exited the car, she had looked off toward the woods in the back of the house. She stood there with her eyes closed, nodding her head softly.

"Oh yes, there is certainly something going on here," she declared upon opening her eyes. "Show me where they are coming from?" Felicity asked encouragingly.

Lee Ann nodded, got up and began walking around the back of the house while Felicity followed behind her. The darkness had increased its opacity so Lee Ann turned on the flashlight on her phone to help guide her through the garden.

"They always come through here. The wildlife preserve is about a quarter of a mile away through the trees on this side of the yard," Lee Ann said, pointing off into the distance.

Felicity closed her eyes again, nodded slightly and then opened them suddenly, her nostrils flaring. "They are close," she announced.

Lee Ann peered into the blackness and saw nothing at first. After her eyes adjusted to the increasing darkness, the soft glow of two, then three dancing orbs began to appear like fireflies in the treetops.

"There . . ." Felicity said.

Lee Ann shivered as Felicity pointed directly at the orbs. They grew closer and descended from the tops of the trees. She made out the now-familiar faces of the middle-aged woman and the man. The third orb then slowly transformed into what appeared to be a black woman, also wearing a nightgown and a bandana. Although it was hard to ascertain every detail of her appearance, she seemed to be young.

Felicity did not move from her location at the edge of the wood as the specter of the white woman appeared beside her. Lee Ann was now standing right next to Felicity. Unlike Lee Ann, Felicity could only sense the energies of these entities and couldn't actually see them.

"Will you help us? They are coming," the woman informed them.

"Who is coming?" Felicity asked her.

"The men from town—the sheriff and the others. Please!" The woman pleaded.

"We can help you but you must stop invading the girl's home," Felicity said firmly. "Lee Ann, close your eyes and take my hand," she said, turning to her side.

Lee Ann did as she was instructed.

"I want you to try and feel the energetic sources around us," she directed. Lee Ann was puzzled about this initially but she knew that she'd perceived such a thing before. At first, when she closed her eyes, there was nothing but darkness. Lee Ann breathed deeply, setting aside all conscious thought and began to open herself to the presences nearby. Like magic, she could perceive the energy of the three figures at the edge of the woods.

"Good, you can feel them for who they really are now. Feel deeper into their presence. Now, I want you to feel the energy like you would feel the wind in your face. Feel how this energy is all around you? Can you feel it?" Felicity asked.

"Yes," Lee Ann uttered shakily. The three figures stopped moving, as if they were waiting for some signal or command from her.

"I want you to let the energy you feel shield you and provide you with a barrier. I want you to create a space away from the house for the presences you sense. A space where they can contact you but cannot pass beyond."

At first, Lee Ann was unsure of how to do this. She searched with her mind and focused on the small storage shed just to their left.

"I found one," she said.

"Good, now try and move your energy toward the surface of your skin and try to hold it there. I know it may seem strange but I need you to try."

Lee Ann gave her a puzzled glance at first but then closed her eyes, knowing that she had to trust in Felicity's instructions. She felt the energy within her and began to try and picture it moving toward the surface of her skin.

"Are you holding that energy in place?" Felicity inquired.

"Yes," Lee Ann replied.

"Good. Feel the energies of the entities present here and try and pull that energy close to you. Now tell them about the boundary," Felicity instructed as she gently touched Lee Ann's arm for support.

"You there in the woods. You may contact me but you may not go beyond the shed. You must not enter my home. You could alarm my parents," she declared, feeling a bit silly giving them this instruction.

"Put aside your conscious mind again; set up the energetic boundary. Reach into your heart and try and connect to love. Picture the light there," Felicity continued. Lee Ann pushed aside her skepticism and tried not to think. Instead she reflected on the love of her mother and father, sensing light growing within her. Slowly, she began to feel the energetic space she was opening just behind them. She even began to sense warmth emanating from it. The others seemed to sense this barrier, too, for they would not move past the boundary.

"Good, you've got it. Now, ask them to reveal what's happened to them."

"Ok, we want to help you. Please tell us why the sheriff and his men are after you," Lee Ann insisted as she opened her eyes and focused on the woman who was only a few feet away from her now. Lee Ann noticed that the figure had turned around to face the complete darkness of the forest behind them.

"No, it's too late. They're here!" The woman wailed in despair, her voice trailing off. The orbs began to retreat toward the west. Lee Ann peered into the woods trying her best to perceive what was there. Felicity's eyes widened and her mouth fell open. She took Lee Ann by the hand and took a step backward.

"What is it? Who's there?" Lee Ann implored, unable to stop her voice from cracking.

"Come away!" Felicity responded. What followed happened so quickly, it seemed almost like a trick of the mind.

Just a few yards into the woods, the glow of what appeared to be the light of several torches appeared. Lee Ann began to hear a sound not unlike the murmur of men's voices. Felicity was now beginning to move further away from the edge of the woods and gripped Lee Ann's hand tighter but she dare not look away.

The voices continued to grow louder. A few yards from the wood's edge, Lee Ann saw what looked to be a translucent sheet with two eye holes that came to a point. It was a lot like a ghost costume she'd created once when she was eight. She swore she could hear the sound of a gun being cocked, then another figure appeared, all clothed in what she could now tell were Klan uniforms. The energetic presence she felt was ominous and overwhelming. All of her being had become filled with the urge to turn and run.

"Stop!" Felicity stretched out her arms and commanded the figures as Lee Ann turned loose of her hand and backed away. This command was answered by a loud shot that seemed to be swallowed by the trees rather than echo the way a normal shot should have.

Lee Ann could no longer hold back the urge to scream, letting it issue forth through the trees as she turned and fled. Felicity was not far behind her. Lee Ann did not turn back to see if the robed figures were following as she ran past the house and down the gravel drive. She was aghast to feel an arm grab her from behind. She tried to pull away but it would not let her go.

"Let me go!" she yelled in fear, turning to see the kindly face of Felicity behind her.

"It's me, Lee Ann. It's just you and me. They've gone," she announced.

"But how do you know?" She asked, struggling to make out anything that might be there in the darkness with them. There was nothing, save the skeletal trunks of the huddled trees on either side of the gravel drive.

"You can tell, just feel," Felicity instructed. It took several moments, but Lee Ann slowly calmed down her beating heart and labored breath before sensing that they were again alone.

For several minutes, Lee Ann was afraid to walk back toward the house.

"It's okay, you've set up a boundary that they will not cross."

"Who were those men? They wanted to harm us, I could feel it!" Lee Ann stated, feeling the goosebumps were beginning to form on her arms again.

"Yes, but you are safe now." It took several minutes for Lee Ann to realize that she was right.

"What happened here was even worse than I thought," Lee Ann said, staring off past the house as if she expected the angry men to set fire to the surrounding woods at any moment, but all was silent. Slowly, they made their way back to the house.

"Yes, I can see that's the case. Whatever happened, those poor souls do not realize that they cannot escape without help. Their fate was decided long ago. Yet to them, there is still a chance to escape their pursuers, to live another day."

"You mean they don't know they've passed on?" Lee Ann asked, puzzled.

"It's possible they do not. It's like a record being stuck on a scratch for years and years, a loop that is played endlessly until someone can pick up the needle and make it stop. That's where you come in."

"But why me? I don't want this ability. I don't want to be afraid all of the time. I . . ."

"Don't want to be overpowered by grief and the fear of living without the support of your mother," Felicity said, as if she had perceived Lee Ann's unvocalized thoughts.

Lee Ann locked eyes with Felicity, feeling the fear draining out of her. Any doubt that she might have felt about this woman's abilities had fled as well. She felt empowered and open to the possibilities with an ally at her side.

"That's better. Open yourself to what you've witnessed. You will be called on again to help them and will be better equipped to handle the task that's been appointed to you. Remember, you are not alone."

Lee Ann realized that it would soon be time for her parents to be returning home. She took out her phone and looked at the time. It was a little after nine.

"My parents will be coming home soon. You have to go before they get back. It wouldn't do for them to find you here. There would be too much explaining to do."

"I know, I'm going to go ahead and leave now. Lee Ann, you have taken an important first step tonight, but there are many more that must be taken. For now, fear not. The energetic barrier will help protect you from the malice that lurks out there."

"Can I tell my friends what we've experienced here tonight? People need to know the truth about what happened here."

"You know in your heart who you can trust and who would be better off not knowing. As far as what happened here, we don't have the full story but it was obviously tragic and much more sinister than what people believe to be true. The full story will be revealed and shared when the time is right. For now, be patient and most importantly, do not fear."

CHAPTER 11
A HOLE IN THE QUIET

Lee Ann woke up and walked slowly down the stairs like she did every morning. Colored streamers hung from the ceiling and balloons lined the hallway and the dining room. There, in the doorway, stood her mother, Kim with her huge, loving smile, and a tray in her hand laden with food.

"My favorite! Blueberry pancakes!!" Lee Ann shouted.

"Happy thirteenth birthday, dear! I want this to be a special day for you. This is only the beginning. We are going to the art gallery in a bit, so I want you to get ready as soon as you're done with your breakfast," Kim instructed, sitting down to take in the joy in her daughter's eyes.

"Mom, you're the best!"

"There's just one thing."

"What's that?" Lee Ann asked, her mouth full of pancakes.

"We are going to have a tiny party later on."

"Mom! I told you I didn't want a party!"

"I know, I know, but your cousins and grandma wouldn't hear of it. They insisted on coming over later tonight. I tried to tell them, but . . ."

"That's okay, mom. I knew it would be impossible to fend off Grandma."

"Just be glad that you have a grandmother in your life that loves and cares about you," Kim's hazel eyes seemed to glass over as she propped up her chin and glanced out of the window, her mind far away for an instant. Lee Ann reached over and put her hand on her mother's wrist, making her smile.

"Mom, I'm so sorry you never got to meet your grandmother. I still don't understand why she disappeared the way she did."

"No one does dear. Your Grandma Jenny was raised by her father after Great Grandma Patricia vanished."

"I wish you could somehow find out why she left. Was she not ready to be a mother or was it something else?" Lee Ann inquired, wondering aloud.

"I used to ask Grandfather Walter about her when I was little but he was always dismissive about it. I think the pain of her leaving was too much for him to recall."

"When did she disappear?"

"Oh gosh, dear, it was decades before I was born, in the fall of 1944, just a couple of years after your Grandma Jenny was born," Kim recalled, her eyes back on the window as if some secret would be uncovered by looking outside.

"I'm sure she had her reasons. I'm sure she never meant to hurt Grandma Jenny," Lee Ann said as she moved in to embrace her mother.

Lee Ann awoke from her dream, sat up, and looked at the pictures of her mother she had faithfully arranged along her antique mirror just as they had been at her old home. The memory and feeling of her mother was so real in that moment. Her experience made it seem as if the dream world and the real world were almost interchangeable. She could again smell her mother's perfume, feel her mother's reassuring touch, and could almost see her mother's encouraging smile.

Then came the crushing pain of realization as Lee Ann's more solid, earthly thoughts reminded her that they would never again share a breakfast like the one they had shared that morning.

Tears flooded Lee Ann's eyes as she embraced her pillow and her memories; however, there was something more to this dream beside the stinging grief and recollection of a past birthday. Her grandmother's disappearance coincided with the events that took place in that beleaguered colony deep in the forest. The timing could have been coincidence, but Lee Ann wasn't sure. This notion lingered in the back of her mind but soon disappeared when she began to recall the events of the night before.

Lee Ann slipped a blue hoodie on over her pajamas and prepared to go downstairs. She began to frame in her mind how she was going to ask her parents' permission to camp out that weekend. However, Lee Ann was much more afraid of the prospect of camping out in that place after what she'd witnessed the night before. The end of the week would mark seventy-four years since the events in the hollow took place. Lee Ann had a notion that it was even more likely that the restless inhabitants there would make their appearance known on the anniversary of the incident. This notion wasn't backed by anything factual; it was just something she knew intuitively.

The presence of Klansmen chasing the women was ominous for Lee Ann, especially when she thought about the story that Jasmine had told her about her grandmother living in the colony. Obviously, these horrid men hiding behind their white sheets held a lot of hatred for these people and Lee Ann wanted to know what the circumstances were behind it all. Felicity's control during the whole series of events had been inspiring and Lee Ann hoped to become as fearless in the face of such phenomena.

In the kitchen, Shirley was standing at the sink like most mornings, gazing out at the forest with a steaming cup of coffee in her hand. Charles had yet to come out of the bedroom. Shirley's forehead creased as she turned to face her stepdaughter.

"Did you not get enough sleep? You look a little worse for wear," Shirley asked. After all of these years, Lee Ann still found Shirley's bluntness a little off-putting.

Why do you have to be that way? Lee Ann wondered.

"Yeah, I didn't sleep well. Not sure why," Lee Ann got up and grabbed her own coffee mug out of the cabinet.

Charles appeared in the doorway of the kitchen, smiling cheerfully.

"Morning, all," he called.

"Morning," Lee Ann answered as she poured her coffee and then added some cream to the steaming cup.

"You alright?" Charles queried, also noticing the deep bags under Lee Ann's eyes, making her look much older than her sixteen years.

"I'm fine. Just more dreams, but that's all they are," she insisted.

"Ok, if you say so," he replied. Charles could tell she was not telling him everything, but he also knew better than to try and pry, knowing he'd find nothing but closed doors. He felt it would best to be patient and let her come to him on her own, so he let it go.

"Dad, I wanted to ask your permission about something." Lee Ann watched as Charles helped himself to the coffee.

"Sure, what's up, hon?"

"I was wondering if I could camp out in the woods with a couple of friends this weekend." Following Lee Ann's request, Shirley's eyes moved to her husband's, narrowing to small slits as if she were willing him to respond a certain way.

"Who are they? I haven't met any of the friends that you've made in school," he responded.

"All I've heard about is these mean girls and about how everyone's such a hick," Shirley added, cocking an eyebrow. Lee Ann shot her a slight glare.

She's going to ruin everything and try and convince dad it's all a bad idea, Lee Ann said to herself

"That's not true. I've told you guys about Katrina and David."

"Well, he certainly can't come. No boys at all, " Shirley insisted. Charles did not respond but he nodded his head in complicity.

"Ok, how about Katrina and Jasmine?" Lee Ann asked.

"Whose this Jasmine? That's the first time I've heard you mention that name," Charles stated.

"Just a new friend from school. She's really nice," Lee Ann said.

"Hmm, I don't see why not, but there's one condition. I want you to bring your friends here first so that we can meet them," Charles declared. Lee Ann's face brightened when he said this.

"You sure about that?" Shirley chimed in, casting a dubious glance in her husband's direction.

"Sure, my parents let me go camping with my friends when I was Lee Ann's age," Charles shared.

"Mmm-hmm, and what did you and your friends get up to when you went camping?" Shirley asked, raising an eyebrow.

"Well, we did some hunting and other things that we won't go into, but overall it was a great way to build friendships. My friends, Bobby and Dave and I were close as three friends could be after bonding like that," Charles added with a guilty smile.

"Is that right?" Lee Ann chided.

"So what's to stop Lee Ann and her friends from getting into similar mischief?" Shirley inquired.

"I trust her. If she says that she wants to have an innocent camping trip with her friends, I believe her," Charles answered. Lee Ann smiled at him, feeling closer than ever to her father. Shirley sighed and turned toward the window; she knew she had lost the argument.

As she walked to school, Lee Ann thought about how she was going to break the news to David that he couldn't go. Although it was tempting to just have him sneak through the woods and meet them, she did not want to betray her father's newly exhibited trust.

Lee Ann was already wrestling with her emotions about not telling her father about Felicity but she knew it was out of the question. Most of the citizens of Laverne were ardent Christians and would likely think that the psychic woman was a new-ager who had no respect for their values. Although her parents weren't religious, Lee Ann had a gut feeling that they wouldn't have confidence in Felicity's abilities and would take away her only lifeline and support she had found to help with the situation.

Lee Ann reached the school grounds. From across the lawn, she spied her nemesis, Mary, talking to Jenn. Ever since the incident in which Lee Ann threw Mary against the lockers, the three tall girls had avoided her, making sure to mutter mean comments and shower her with looks of disdain in passing. Lee Ann smiled at them as they whispered something and glared at her. It was obvious they were too afraid to continue to bully her or Katrina to the extent that they had before. Nonetheless, the three friends relished any opportunity to make a snide comment, if only to reinforce the rumors they had spread about

Lee Ann—that she had belonged to a gang or a rock band when she lived in Nashville. Someone even suggested that she had been kicked out of her last school for fighting. Some of these rumors had gotten back to Lee Ann, making her laugh in amusement.

As soon as she got inside the building, she found Katrina at her locker, dressed in a black t-shirt and wearing her favorite black and white checkered skirt with black tights.

"Hey! Did you get your parents' permission to campout?" she inquired immediately.

"Yes, but I don't know how to break it to David that he can't go," Lee Ann said.

"Well, it's no surprise to me that they didn't want any boys to come. My dad would have been mortified."

"I didn't even bother fighting them about it. I knew it was futile," Lee Ann added. Jasmine walked toward them, wearing a purple headband, matching converse sneakers, and purple tights. Jasmine had finally found friends that shared her sense of fashion.

"Hi!" Jasmine said in her friendly, shy manner.

"Hey!" Lee Ann and Katrina answered simultaneously.

Jasmine drug her left foot across the floor slightly and bit her bottom lip the way she did when she was feeling a bit shy. Ever since she'd started high school, she'd been looking for a peer group that she fit in with. Now, she had found what she felt was the perfect group, and she was thinking carefully about her words, wanting to make a good impression.

"Any news about Thief's Hollow?" Jasmine inquired.

"Well, my parents have given me permission to have friends come and camp out on our land. You have got to come. Maybe we can find out more about what's happening out there. Do you think you can join us?"

"I'm sure my mom will probably say yes but I will definitely ask tonight," Jasmine's face lit up.

"This is going to be such an exciting camping trip!" Katrina blurted out.

"Shh!" Lee Ann said, noticing that David was making his way toward them.

"What? You're going to have to tell him anyway," Katrina insisted.

"Tell me what?" David asked, rushing up beside Katrina.

"My dad says that we can go camping but no boys allowed," Lee Ann shared.

"Well, duh, what did you expect he was going to say? You've got to learn to lie to your parents from time to time," David lectured.

"Maybe I don't want to," Lee Ann said, creasing her forehead.

"Come on, everybody does it sometimes," he insisted.

Lee Ann didn't respond. Ever since she'd met David, she was unsure of her feelings for him. She knew that she was attracted to him, but there was something that kept her from wanting to actually go out with him. What added to her uncertainty about her feelings was this air of flippancy he had like a lot of boys his age, their insistence that nothing was to be taken too seriously.

Sensing that she wasn't going to come around to his point of view, David reversed course.

"Ok, I won't come if that's what you want," he declared as the excitement ran from his face. Lee Ann felt sorry for him in that moment.

"Thank you for understanding," she said, giving him a hug. He quickly turned and walked off down the hallway to try and hide the disappointment on his face.

"David, wait . . ." Lee Ann called after him but he had already ducked into a classroom.

"He'll get over it, don't worry," Katrina consoled, but Lee Ann stood outside the classroom with a forlorn look on her face. David had been supportive of her this whole time and it seemed unfair for him to be excluded based on his gender. She turned to face Katrina and Jasmine who were standing just behind her.

"Why should he be excluded just because he's a boy? Do they think he's going to try and make out with all of us or what?" Lee Ann asked in her frustration.

"Typical parent stuff. They just want what they think is best," Jasmine said, trying to reassure her. Lee Ann smiled at her, feeling comfort from the support.

"Maybe, but it's still not fair," she replied and proceeded down the hall to her own class.

The time was set for six to meet up the following evening at Lee Ann's house. Lee Ann texted Felicity to tell her about their plan. Felicity texted back that she would meet up with them at the site of the colony a bit later.

As night drew its curtain over twilight, Lee Ann stared out of her window at the storage shed adjacent to the garden. She wondered if the energetic barrier that had been set up would be respected by the lost souls bound to this stretch of wilderness. Before long, she spied the orbs dancing in the treetops, moving closer to the edge of the woods. Curiosity got the better of Lee Ann and she decided to see what else she could find out from the spirits. She checked to make sure her parents' bedroom door was closed, tiptoed down the stairs, grabbed her coat, and gently closed the backdoor, making her way toward the shed.

The shed door creaked open, revealing a dusty shelf covered with long unused tools, such as a rusty spade and a dulled ax. She sat down on a small wooden bench next to the shelf, facing the doorway, which faced the woods. It wasn't long before a bluish orb descended from the treetops and became the now-familiar transparent figure of the middle-aged woman, eyes wide with desperation.

"Please help! They will kill us if you don't!" the woman implored as she slowly took a step inside of the shed.

Don't worry. You've set up a boundary. The familiar, motherly voice reassured her. Lee Ann wanted to ask questions but she was anxious to talk with the troubled woman.

"How can I help you? What you think is going to happen to you has already happened," Lee Ann tried to explain. The look of confusion and pain on the woman's face showed that she didn't understand. That's when it dawned on Lee Ann that it would be hard to make these poor souls understand what had befallen them.

"The men are coming. Something must be done to stop them before they kill more people!" the woman shrieked.

"Who are you? What is your name?" Lee Ann asked, noticing that three orbs were now lining up in front of the door, slowly materializing into the transparent shapes of people.

"Carolyn Gracie," the woman declared.

"Carolyn, I don't know how to tell you this, but you are . . . Uh, that is to say, you and the others have already, um . . . died," Lee Ann stammered.

Hearing this, the woman was aghast with shock and disbelief.

"No, no, you don't understand. They are coming!" the woman urgently repeated. Lee Ann shook her head, unsure of what else to say.

Behind Carolyn was the same man she'd previously seen but his features were now in sharper focus. He looked to be about the same age as Carolyn, his hair thin and short. He wore tattered overalls and a collared shirt, full of holes.

"Bobby, explain to this young lady what's going on . . ." Carolyn implored as the man entered the shed behind her.

"Please listen to what my wife is saying. They mean to kill us. We've managed to stay hidden for quite some time, but they've found us," the man explained, pleading.

"It's been longer than months, I assure you," Lee Ann insisted, not knowing if she could make them understand their fate. Just as she started to ask more questions, she saw three more orbs appear; beyond these, torchlight and a flash of translucent white from the cloaks of the Klansmen in the distance. The soft breeze rattled the sparse leaves of the trees and was soon overcome by the sound of angry men's voices and the bay of a hound.

"We're too late!" Carolyn said as she and her husband disappeared from the entrance of the shed. Lee Ann's fear returned and the desire to leave tugged at her. However, a part of her wanted to stay in the shed to test the boundaries she and Felicity had set up.

Lee Ann exited the shed and quickly made her way toward the backdoor of the house to see what else she could safely glimpse in the darkness. The orbs had begun to drift further away but the torchlight became brighter and the voices louder. Lee Ann was overwhelmed by the sense of a great malice emanating from the woods.

"They went this way, Jim!" a voice called out. Lee Ann could now clearly see six of the klansmen emerging from the woods; the last one had a hound on a leash. They stopped just short of the shed as if they sensed something barring their way. Lee Ann slowly opened the door, unable to stop her trembling. As she entered the house, she saw one of the men take aim at one of the orbs and a single shot ripped a hole in the quiet of the night. Lee Ann's hands leapt to her mouth and stifled her scream as the backdoor quietly closed behind her.

For several minutes, she sat on the stairs, staring in the direction of the back garden. After a while, she went back into the kitchen and peered out of the window. All was quiet and nothing stirred except a few brown leaves kicked up by the wind.

CHAPTER 12
SLIGHT REVEAL

I t was difficult for Lee Ann to get to sleep that night. The events of the evening had revealed more pieces of the puzzle, but in the end what she experienced just created yet more questions. Her restless mind pondered these mysteries, which drowned out any sad memories or vivid dreams of her mother that had been invading her sleep.

Lee Ann's initial confusion had grown into urgency and fascination but her fear still remained.

With each experience of this supernatural phenomena, Lee Ann saw the figures more vividly. The details of the figures, although still translucent, were more sharply focused with each new encounter.

That morning, Lee Ann sat up, glancing over at her sketchbook by the bedside table that hadn't seen much use lately. Inspired, she sketched the figures emerging from the woods. She took her time and added as much detail as she could remember, particularly with Carolyn Gracie.

When she began to sketch the sharp outline of the ghost-like klan robes, she felt a sudden current of dread run through her body. She dropped the sketchbook to the ground, closed her eyes and sighed.

I'll get back to that one day.

Passing by her discarded sketchbook, she hurried to her computer to research the name the woman had revealed to her: Carolyn Gracie. There were all sorts of things that popped up but nothing that seemed to match the circumstances she had seen with the orbs. Finally, when she was about to give up, she found a discussion thread called *Haunted Happenings* and decided to anonymously post a question about the legend of Thief's Hollow:

Does anyone have any information about the legend of Thief's Hollow in middle Tennessee? I have reason to believe that the events used to describe the 'hauntings' occurring there are false. In particular, does anyone know anything about a Carolyn Gracie? I have reason to believe she is connected with the events that took place. Thank you!

She posted her question to the forum and went downstairs to brew some coffee. She was relieved to see that Shirley and her father were still asleep. She dreaded the idea of having another discussion about where she was off to. Just as the coffee was done, Shirley appeared in the doorway, still wearing her nightgown.

"Well this is a first—you got up before me," Shirley smiled, smelling the coffee.

"I woke up and remembered that I had to finish a project for history, so I'm about to go to the library again," Lee Ann stated casually.

Shirley lifted her eyebrows and looked her stepdaughter up and down.

"You're still trying to find out about Thief's Hollow, aren't you?" Shirley said in her blunt manner.

Lee Ann sighed and came clean. "Yes, I am."

"Why didn't you just say that?" Shirley asked.

Lee Ann turned to the cabinet and got down two coffee mugs.

"Because I didn't want you and dad to worry that I was becoming obsessed with the legend. I just want to get to the bottom of what happened out there. I believe the legend isn't true," she insisted.

"Based on what, exactly?"

"I can't explain. It's just a hunch."

"Come on, Lee Ann. Give me a little bit of credit. I know you well enough by now to see when you're not being straight with me. I want you to know that you can come to me—about anything."

Lee Ann smiled. It was the first time Shirley had said anything like this to her before and she appreciated it.

"I want you to know something too," Lee Ann answered.

"Ok, shoot," Shirley replied.

"I'm not in a battle with you for dad's attention." As soon as the words left Lee Ann's mouth, she was surprised she'd said them but it was, in fact, something that she'd wanted to say for some time.

Shirley crossed her arms, relaxed the tense lines in her face and smiled.

"I know," she said simply. At that moment, Lee Ann wanted to reach out to her the way she might have with her mother but it was a good enough start for them to share this moment without that closeness. Besides, like Lee Ann, Shirley was not the touchy-feely type. Even though Lee Ann had grown away from this stubborn separation from others with the support of her new friends, she didn't want to press her luck with Shirley.

"So, are you going to tell me why you think this legend is false?"

"Only if you promise not to freak out and send me to the psych ward."

Shirley laughed as Lee Ann poured some coffee into one of the mugs and handed it to her. Lee Ann heard a soft shuffle and realized her father was standing outside the kitchen listening.

"How long have you been lingering there, Dad?" Her words prompted Shirley to turn and face him.

"Long enough," he said with a smile. "Alright, so let's hear it! I know you've been trying to hide it but I could tell that you've been preoccupied with this ghost story."

"Ok, so here's the deal. You're going to have to suspend some disbelief. First off, neither one of you thinks I'm crazy, right?"

"Of course not," Charles insisted.

"Shirley?" Lee Ann asked, turning to her stepmother.

"No, Lee Ann."

"Ok, well, I've already told you about the voices I'd been hearing. Well, things have gotten more intense. I've actually seen people—or the spirits of people—out there in the woods." She decided to skip the part about them entering the house for now, not wanting to scare them too much. She also decided not to mention the reassuring voice that she'd been hearing in her head. At this point she didn't want to give them any additional reasons to think she might be going crazy.

Shirley and Charles looked at each other, both of them trying to gauge how the other was taking this news.

"What—or who—did you see, exactly?" Charles inquired.

"I saw a middle-aged woman in a nightgown and a man, about the same age. There were others that I couldn't get as close a look at that followed behind them. The first woman even told me her name: Carolyn Gracie."

Again, Shirley and Charles exchanged glances, only this time, their expressions were much more confused.

"Ok, never heard of her. What else happened?" Shirley inquired.

"There were men dressed in Klan robes and one of them had a dog. They were obviously chasing the others. These spirits have been trying to get me to help them."

"Are you sure that you didn't have a dream or somethin' that seemed like it was real at the time?" Charles questioned, moving in closer to his daughter. He was doing his best to give her the benefit of the doubt but his skepticism was taking hold.

"Yes, I'm sure, Dad," she insisted.

"I don't know what to say, pumpkin'. I mean, put yourself in our position. How would all this sound to you, if the shoe were on the other foot?" Charles asked, shaking his head.

"Trust me, I know it sounds crazy. I didn't ask for any of this to happen but it is happening and trying to deny it or call it some trick of the mind hasn't stopped it. Somehow, I have to help those people. For some reason, I have some connection to what happened there and they're seeking me out. I have to find out what really happened and free them from this loop they're stuck in."

"I have heard the voices," Shirley said out of the blue, prompting a look from Charles.

"What?" he asked with astonishment.

"Yeah. The first time I thought it was the wind or that I was dreaming but then I heard it again just last night. There was a gunshot, too," Shirley added.

Lee Ann's face lit up as she heard her stepmother admit these things.

"Yes, there was! That was one of the Klansmen! They are trying to kill the people who need my help, although I suspect that they killed them many years ago. The tragedy that occurred out there keeps repeating itself; it's like living through the same nightmare over and over again." Lee Ann struggled to explain what she barely understood herself.

If only Felicity could be here now, Lee Ann thought to herself.

"Well, I must admit that I don't know what to make of everything you've told us, but I do know that there's something going on here. I could tell when we first moved in here. All the same, I've never been one to believe in ghosts and legends," Shirley admitted.

"Why didn't you say somethin'?" Charles asked. He was still recovering from his initial shock.

"For the same reason Lee Ann didn't want to come to us about what's been happening to her. It sounds flat out insane!" Shirley shook her head and sighed.

"Look, I'm not asking you to blindly accept anything or fully understand what's happening. I don't either. What I need from you guys is your support while I try and find out what's going on. I need for you to let me get to the bottom of this."

Lee Ann watched as Shirley and Charles stared at one another for a long while; she wondered what the two of them were thinking, hoping that they'd be supportive.

"Ok, Lee Ann, you have our support," Shirley asserted. Charles frowned at his wife, as if she were going too far.

"But please be careful. I don't want you scaring yourself out there in the woods tonight. Why don't you let me come with you?" Charles asked as he put his hand gently on her shoulder.

"Dad, no. I don't know if you're ready to experience what might be awaiting us there."

"You need an adult with you."

"Ok, now that I'm coming clean about everything I might as well tell you that I have had some adult help with this situation," Lee Ann confessed.

"Really?" Charles sounded a bit annoyed as he exchanged another glance with Shirley. "Who?"

"Felicity Taylor."

"The town psychic? Come on, Lee Ann," Charles chided, unable to stop himself from laughing.

"I met her in the library when I was doing some research. Dad, she's the real deal. She told me that I was like a beacon in the darkness attracting these souls. She recognized that I had the gift that she possesses—the ability to see a world beyond our own and to help those that need to transition or crossover. Just the other night she helped me to set up a barrier so these souls won't enter our home. Guys, the woman I mentioned was in our laundry room!" Shirley cast a frightened glance in the direction of the small room to her right.

"Now, they are only able to meet with me in the shed out back or in the woods."

Charles was overwhelmed and confused. He simply shook his head and sighed.

"I don't know what to say, Lee Ann. You've never lied to me before, so I believe that you believe in all of these things. I'll let you go out there and seek the answers that you're looking for but if you encounter any trouble or even just get scared, I want you to text or call me right away. The signal is weak out here but should be strong enough. In fact . . . I'm going to give you a walkie-talkie in case the phone signal dies or doesn't work."

"Ok, Dad. We're just going to be a few miles away in the wildlife preserve," Lee Ann reassured him. "For now, I'm going to go and see what I can find out about Carolyn at the library."

"Ok, Lee," Charles answered. After Lee Ann grabbed her coat and left the house, the two of them stood there in silence, taking in what Lee Ann had told them, unsure of how to process it or what to do next.

The library was virtually empty except for the bespectacled librarian who, as far as Lee Ann knew, was always there.

"Back again, are we?" The librarian was glad to see someone there.

"Yes ma'am."

"Still researching local legends?" She went on to ask.

"Yes, I'm trying to look up information about a specific person," Lee Ann revealed, wondering how much she should tell the woman.

"Oh? Might I ask who?"

"Carolyn Gracie," Lee Ann admitted. As soon as the name left her mouth, she saw a look of recognition flash across the woman's face.

"Have you heard of her?" Lee Ann asked encouragingly.

"Yes, I believe I have in passing, although I can't recall where or when I heard the name. I do know that the Gracies no longer live in this area."

"Really?" Lee Ann's face lit up and her pupils widened.

"Yes, I'm afraid I don't know much else. Seems like her family left back in the forties, although I must confess I'm not quite old enough to remember the specifics. I was only a very little girl at the time."

"I see. Did any other people, um, leave around that same time that you can recall?"

"Yes, I believe a couple of other families left then, although I can't recall their names or the circumstances. So many have come and gone over the years," she said with a smile.

Lee Ann smiled back, trying to determine if the woman was telling her everything she knew or was hiding something. Unsure, Lee Ann turned away and walked to the local section, feeling the librarian's eyes follow her steps.

"Let me know if you need any help, dear," the librarian offered as her usually helpful demeanor returned.

Lee Ann found records of vital statistics that showed Carolyn Gracie was, in fact, a real person. She also discovered that she was an activist who had launched a canvassing group to promote local candidates in the late thirties who were in favor of workers' and civil rights, as evidenced by a local newspaper article entitled, "Local Woman Gets Out the Vote." After about an hour, she was unable to ascertain any further information, so Lee Ann gave up. She also tried to look up information about her great grandmother, only to find that the library held little or no information about Patricia, other than the typical record of her vital statistics.

Looking at her phone, she realized that the afternoon was waning. It would be time to meet up with the others for the camp out in just a couple of hours.

"Did you find anything else out?" The librarian asked as Lee Ann emerged from the local section.

"A little bit," Lee Ann shared, sounding deflated. She was unsure how much she trusted this woman. She thought about asking about her great-grandmother, Patricia Mulberry, but something kept her from doing so.

Be patient, Lee Ann. It's all coming together. She tried to reassure herself as she walked back home. The town receded behind her as trees took over the landscape on either side of the road as if they were leaning to be let in on a secret. The clouds amassed above her, indicating that it was going to be a dark night with veiled stars.

Lee Ann packed her backpack and threw the walkie-talkie her father had given her into the side pocket. Not long after she was ready, Katrina and Jasmine appeared at her front door. Both of them were dressed warmly in sweaters, jackets, and scarves to protect against the elements.

"Hello there, girls," Charles greeted warmly. Shirley, who didn't smile often, did her best to be friendly, welcoming them in.

"Come on in. I'll make you some hot chocolate, if you like," Shirley offered. Lee Ann came down the stairs, surprised to hear her step-mother being so motherly.

"Hey guys. This is Jasmine and Katrina, the friends of mine from school I mentioned," Lee Ann shared.

"Pleased to meet you. I'm Charles and this is my wife, Shirley." Charles extended his hand to the girls who gave him a friendly smile in return.

"Good to meet you, sir," Katrina said. Jasmine, being a bit more shy, just smiled and shook his hand.

Lee Ann ran up to them with a huge smile on her face. She was happy to have her friends by her side for what could prove to be a very frightening evening ahead.

"I see you've brought plenty of supplies," Lee Ann joked with

Katrina, seeing a large grocery bag in her hands, in addition to the pack stuffed to the gills on Katrina's back.

"Yep, my dad says you can never have enough provisions in the wilderness. By provisions, of course I mean snacks and food. I've got hot dogs, hamburgers, and stuff to make s'mores," Katrina said, looking pleased with herself.

"As long as you understand that it's a three mile hike and you'll have to carry it the whole way," Lee Ann stated, causing Katrina's mouth to fall open.

"Don't worry, we'll help you," Jasmine said, reassuringly, her mouth curving to a smile. Lee Ann thought about how pretty Jasmine's smile was and how much she wanted to get to know this shy member of their group better. She also hoped that Jasmine would find answers about her family's past.

"Remember, Lee Ann: if you need anything, anything at all, you know what to do, hon," Charles reminded her. Lee Ann smiled and hugged her father.

"Of course I do, but don't worry, Dad." Then her eyes shifted to Shirley and without thinking, Lee Ann went over and hugged her too. Shirley, taken by surprise, smiled and put her arms around her step-daughter. Charles was elated; it was the first time he'd seen the two of them embrace.

Shirley and Charles stood on the back porch and watched as the group of friends made their way past the storage shed and garden, now cleared of the brown tangled weeds that once engulfed it, until they crossed the stream and disappeared into the deep forest.

"I still think I should have insisted on going with them," Charles said as he slipped his hand around Shirley's waist.

"No, she has to do this on her own, Charles. Let her go," Shirley said, showing a new empathy toward Lee Ann that surprised him.

Charles turned toward her, kissing her on the cheek. Despite his confusion over the things his daughter had revealed to them that morning, he felt his family was now more of a unit. Before, it had felt as if they were running a boarding house with a teenage guest that neither of them really knew. Now he truly felt like they were cementing a stronger bond.

CHAPTER 13
THE HEART OF THE MATTER

Itt was nearing twilight by the time the group came to the sign
that marked the boundary of the wildlife preserve.

"I have to admit this is the first time I've ever been camping,"
Jasmine revealed.

"Really? Well, normally I'd say you were in for a treat but this could
prove to be a bit more, eh, interesting than your average camping trip,"
Lee Ann said.

"Hey, we've got each other, right? Besides, how many documented
cases are there where some supernatural entity actually harmed a
human being?" Katrina remarked. No one answered her attempt at
comforting them because no one really knew the answer, and that
proved unsettling.

"How much farther is it?" Katrina asked, changing the subject.

"About three miles in or so," Lee Ann answered.

"When is Felicity meeting up with us?" Jasmine asked.

"She said that she would make every effort to meet up with us
before dark, so I expect she will be along any minute."

As if on cue, the rustle and crunch of leaves sounded in the direction from which they had come.

"Someone's coming, I hope it's Felicity," Jasmine said nervously.

"Don't worry, I'm sure that it's her," Lee Ann stated, but after the things she'd experienced out there, she wasn't at all sure.

"Who's there?" Katrina called out, trying to appear brave. A figure dressed in a long, black coat, purple scarf and hiking boots appeared above them on the hill they had just traversed. There was an unnerving moment when everyone was uncertain as to the identity of the person.

"I hope I haven't kept you waiting," the kindly voice of Felicity broke the tension and brought a welcome relief to the nervous group as she made her way down the slope toward them.

"No, no. We were just pausing for a moment," Lee Ann said, giving the woman a hug after she caught up with them. "Everyone, this is Felicity Taylor, a friend of mine. Felicity, this is Jasmine and Katrina."

"My pleasure," Felicity greeted, respectfully shaking each of their hands while revealing her motherly, pleasant smile. Her strong, supportive presence immediately brightened the mood of the group.

"Very nice to meet you," Katrina uttered in a friendly, almost relieved tone.

"Likewise," Jasmine said, more shyly.

"We're losing light fast so we had best be on our way. It gets harder to find the path in total darkness," Lee Ann warned.

"So, Ms. Taylor, what is it that we can expect to find out here tonight?" Katrina asked.

"Please, call me Felicity. That, my dear friends, is a good question. One thing for certain is that we needn't come way out here to establish contact with these souls. They are actively seeking out Lee Ann."

"Then why come all the way out here?" Katrina asked bluntly.

"Well, in order for us to gain a better understanding about what took place here and how we can help those who were involved, we are going to the heart of the disturbance," Felicity revealed.

"So, why are they seeking her out?" Katrina continued.

"Hmm, I'm not entirely sure; though I do know that she possesses a rare sensitivity to this world parallel to our own, the spiritual plane. You see, the souls that dwell there give off energy fields, much as the living do. Truth be told, all of us have the ability to perceive and manipulate certain energies but over the passage of time we have forgotten how to see, if you will. The reason most of us have lost the ability to perceive these energies is because we are preoccupied with so many other things in the modern world. So-called 'primitive' humans were more tuned into this realm and the cycles of nature," Felicity explained.

"Oh," Katrina said, trying to take all of this in.

"Inquisitiveness is part of what has been lost. Yours will certainly serve you well," Felicity said, turning to face Katrina who was walking just behind her. Katrina smiled back.

"Inquisitive is a good word; some have called me mouthy and nosey," Katrina confided.

"Do not let people turn your assets into faults. That is a sign of their own insecurities," Felicity answered.

"That's what I always suspected," Katrina boasted with more than an air of snark, inspiring laughter from the others.

They entered the hollow where Lee Ann had turned back the first time she ventured into the preserve. Suddenly, they heard footsteps about a hundred yards off to their right but the trees would not reveal the source of the sound.

"Shh!' Lee Ann said, making a hand motion to indicate the group should stop moving and listen. The group went silent behind her, anticipating some ominous presence that would soon reveal itself. Katrina and Jasmine crouched down behind Lee Ann while Felicity peered into the space to make out the source of the footsteps.

"Reveal yourself," Felicity commanded. The hearts of the others jumped as a figure stepped out from behind a tree, now only about ten yards away.

"Hey, there," David called out, walking toward them, wearing a rather large backpack.

"Oh my god David, you scared the crap out of us," Katrina crowed.

"Sorry, didn't mean to. I thought I was making enough noise so I wouldn't surprise you. Besides, ghosts don't make noise when they walk through the woods, do they?" he asked, turning towards Felicity.

"David, I thought I told you that you couldn't come?" Lee Ann scolded.

"Sorry, I just couldn't let you guys come out here on your own. I want to help. Besides, what your parents don't know won't hurt them."

Lee Ann couldn't be mad at him. Secretly, she felt comforted by his presence.

"I'm David, by the way," he said, extending his hand to Felicity.

"Nice to meet you, young man, I'm—" she went to answer but he finished for her.

"You're Felicity, the psychic. Everyone knows who you are."

"I don't know if that's a good thing or not. I know what most people say about me," she remarked, shaking his hand and looking deeply into his eyes.

"Well, if we're going on a ghost hunt, I can't think of anyone else more qualified to help," he joked.

"Hmm, yes, well you don't need me to provide you with a window to the beyond. Lee Ann here possesses that same ability," she declared.

The group soon fell silent again as the twilight faded into the gathering darkness. They had reached the gently sloping hill above the fabled hollow; Lee Ann hesitated here for a moment.

"That's the place, down there," she pointed out.

"So, let's go! No place that I haven't been," David said briefly, but the others paused, looking over at Felicity who had closed her eyes.

"Yes, this is the place. So much hurt and fear. So much hatred and unsettled energy," she asserted as a single tear trickled down her cheek. "Can you feel it?" she asked them softly.

Lee Ann was attempting to be strong for the others but she, too, felt the pressure. What she experienced was much like the oppression animals often feel before an impending storm. She felt overwhelmed, the same way she had when she and David visited the place before. Only this time, she was determined to overcome her fear and be strong for the group.

"Yes, I can feel it," Lee Ann said simply. The urge to turn and run came and went like a sudden breeze blowing by.

"Let us go forward. Be strong everyone!" Felicity encouraged, pausing to take Lee Ann's hand in her own before moving forward again. Behind Felicity and Lee Ann came Katrina, who stayed close to them, rubbing her hands to warm herself. Jasmine stayed close to David, who brought up the rear of the group.

In the very last of the fading light, the group reached the bottom of the hill. There lay the stone foundation and, to its right, the pile of rotting timbers that once was a barn. Felicity closed her eyes again, seeing a vision of a burning building that came and went. She swore, for an instant, she could even smell the fire.

"You okay?" Katrina asked Felicity.

"Yes, the place is revealing some of its story. Come, let's find a suitable place to make camp before the light leaves us entirely," she entreated.

The group had very little desire to make camp so close to the site, so they chose a level site near a small spring creek, within view of the site, about sixty yards away. David helped Lee Ann unpack and set up the large dome tent that her mother had bought for her two years prior. Setting up the structure reminded Lee Ann of her mother and their last camping trip together to the Ozarks. It had rained while they were on a hike and the two of them laughed as they ran for the shelter of the tent together.

"You okay?" David asked her just after he staked the last tent pole into the hard ground.

"Yep, this just takes me back to the last time I used this tent. I was with my mother," she shared.

"Cherish that memory. Do not let it fill your heart with sadness," Felicity suddenly said from behind her. Lee Ann didn't answer but smiled instead. However, even with Felicity's support the fleeting joy of her memory was chased away by the all too familiar sense of loss, even abandonment.

Once the tent was set up, David began to gather pieces of wood for the fire. He had even brought a small hatchet that he used to chop up a large oak branch. Soon, a good-sized pile of wood had been gathered. David dusted off his hands, went over to his backpack and brought out several camp chairs that he passed around to the others. Lee Ann also brought out a couple of chairs from her pack. Soon, the fire was going and they were all seated around it, some cooking hotdogs on sticks while others waited for the burgers that David had put on a portable grill he'd set up over the fire.

"Quite the prepared camper, aren't you?" Felicity commented as she pulled her gray shawl to shield herself from the cool air that began to descend into the hollow.

"Been a few hundred times or so, usually on huntin' trips with my dad and uncle."

"Guess you've never been on a hunt like this," she remarked.

"No ma'am, but I have to say I'm excited about it!"

Felicity smiled at him and looked over at Jasmine, who'd been very quiet since they'd set up camp, her eyes gazing over in the direction of the remains of the colony to their west.

"You have a connection to this place too, do you not?" Felicity surmised.

"Yes, my grandmother lived here when she was very young," Jasmine replied.

"What has she told you?"

"She doesn't like to talk about it. Every time I ask her questions, she promises to tell me everything that she can remember when I am old enough." Something about Felicity's warm and friendly demeanor made Jasmine want to open up.

"I see. All will be revealed in time. Be patient," Felicity reassured her.

"I hope so. I don't know quite how to say this, but it's almost as if this whole haunting or whatever you want to call it hangs over this town like some kind of curse," Jasmine added. The others looked at her curiously, but David and Katrina both nodded slightly like they had some idea what she meant. Felicity nodded as well.

"Yes, it's true. I could sense it when I first came to live here as well. It was like there was a shameful secret that no one talked about or was even sure about but the effect of it was palpable. Some of my clients, especially those who had lived in Laverne all of their lives, described a kind of weight or oppression that they felt. One of them was a hunter who had spent a considerable amount of time in this area," Felicity described.

"Yep. I've heard similar things. I've also felt that something was hanging over the town—like a storm coming on. That feeling along with the mixed opinions I've heard about Thief's Hollow let me know something was up with this place," David acknowledged. A long pause followed as everyone let all of this sink in, each of them lost in their own thoughts.

"So, why hasn't anything happened yet? I mean, we're out here and the sun's gone down, but I don't hear or see a thing," David wondered aloud, breaking the silence.

"It's not time yet," Lee Ann answered as she stared blankly into the fire.

"Every time the spirits reveal themselves, it's around eight o' clock. I noticed that the last time."

"Yes, you see, whatever befell the people who lived here is playing itself out night after night at a specific time on endless repeat. It's kind of like a tape loop—it plays over and over again," Felicity disclosed just as the distant baying of coyotes could be heard coming from somewhere out of the east.

Jasmine and Katrina both shivered at the sound, moving their chairs in closer to each other and the fire, which David fed with two more logs.

"Why does that happen, though? Why won't those people go on to whatever awaits them in the afterlife?" Katrina asked.

"Well, it usually happens when there's some trauma associated with the deceased. We know the people that lived here met a terrible fate because it left its mark on this place. Also, it could very well be that the people that died here don't even fully realize what had happened to them. They need someone to free them from the loop and guide them on to the next plane of existence. They are holding on to some aspect of their lives that is keeping them from seeing the way forward," Felicity paused as she carefully selected the next thing to say to them.

"Have you helped people, eh, find their way to the next plane?" Katrina asked.

"Yes," she said as the firelight illuminated her smile.

"So, you are going to help these souls find their way?" Jasmine asked.

"Lee Ann will help them," Felicity stated reassuringly.

"But I have no idea how," Lee Ann answered and she switched her attention from the firelight toward the site of the colony. She turned her gaze from the direction of the ruined buildings and locked eyes with Felicity whose face took on a certain angelic quality in the firelight.

"Neither did I at first. Neither do most who possess such sensitivities," Felicity reassured her.

Lee Ann's downward curved mouth expressed her mixed confusion and frustration.

"So, Ms. Felicity, I have to ask. What's it like being a psychic? I mean, how did you get into the business?" David asked after swallowing a bite of hot dog. His question lightened the mood slightly.

"I've been practicing for about twenty years now. I was a teacher before that, over in Hohenwald," she revealed.

"What did you teach?" Jasmine asked.

"Science, actually."

"Why did you quit?" Katrina queried.

"It's a long story, but let's just say that people found out about my abilities and began to ostracize me. Some even said I was a witch. I just got tired of it and left town."

"When did you first know that you had a gift?" Katrina asked.

"My, you all are inquisitive, aren't you? Well, my gifts, as you so aptly call them, began to reveal themselves long ago, when I was only a bit older than you all. I had strange dreams and visions, which I didn't read much into at first. However, I soon realized that actual souls were trying to contact me. I was standing in an old Catholic church with my mother when I got the strangest feeling—I felt the presence of a sad woman. From that, I was compelled to walk into the confession booth. I could not see her but I could feel her energy. I experienced her sadness as if her emotions were my own. Something intuitive compelled me to communicate with her through my thoughts and feelings. She told me that she had confessed her sins in the very spot where I stood and afterward had taken her own life."

"How awful," Jasmine whispered.

"Yes, it was. She was the first person that I tried to help. It took me awhile before I thought I actually knew what to do."

"What did you do?" Lee Ann entreated, hoping that Felicity would reveal some tricks of the trade in that moment.

"You will know soon enough. You have to find a way to help untie the attachments that these souls have to this existence; help them to let go of what keeps them trapped in between the two planes." A thick blanket of calm fell over the group as they took in Felicity's words. It subdued them all until Katrina's natural and lively inquisitiveness broke the silence.

"So, why did you choose to move to Laverne when you left Hohenwald? Weren't you afraid that you'd have the same experience all over again in another small town?" Katrina inquired.

"One cannot escape one's origins completely. I could have moved to the other side of the country and I would still feel the pull of my home. Besides, my mother lived here and I wanted to be close to her. She died a few years ago but I expect I will now stay."

"But why stay in a town that thinks you're a phony? No offense, but people talk and most of the adults I've heard from think your business is a racket," David revealed.

Felicity laughed at this. "David, I appreciate your honesty. I know what people say about me but after so many years I can say that it no longer bothers me. Truth be told, many of the people who tell others I'm a phony have secretly sought out my help. You would be surprised who has asked for my services."

"Who, please tell us, who?" Katrina, Jasmine, and David all asked at once.

"Now, now, I will not betray the confidentiality of my clients. Let's just say that people don't always believe what they tell others in public. In a town like Laverne, it doesn't usually play out well if you speak your mind and it doesn't jive with popular opinion."

"So you mean some of these church-goers are secretly getting tarot card and palm readings?" Katrina quizzed as her eyes widened.

"And other things. Some want to know how their loved ones are making out in the afterlife. Some want to know their own fate, which I cannot fully know. All that is revealed to me in such instances are clues that the client reveals through their energy," Felicity shared.

"If my dad could see me now, hangin' with the town psychic. He'd give me a proper scolding, he would," David chortled as he reached for a marshmallow to put on the end of the branch he'd just used to cook his hotdog.

"On top of that, you're camping out with three girls," Lee Ann added.

"He wouldn't care about that nearly as much, I promise you," he responded with a sly grin.

The others laughed at this, but this was soon interrupted by a noise coming from the direction of the old buildings' remains. It sounded like a mournful female voice.

"What . . . what was that?" Katrina asked as she moved in closer to Jasmine seeking comfort.

"It's time," Lee Ann said as she looked at the clock on her cell phone, which read that the time was seven fifty-nine. There was also a message from Charles:

Everything alright, hun?

So far, so good, dad, she answered, not wanting him to worry.

The sound, which seemed to be a cry at first, soon became a call for help. It was the same woman's voice that Lee Ann first heard in the woods behind her house.

"Help us!" the voice called out again, causing David to move in front of the girls and stare out into the gloom. Lee Ann got to her feet and moved over by David. Katrina and Jasmine now both had their arms tightly wound around each other, shivering as they stared in the direction of the disembodied voice.

"Stay close, everyone," Felicity said, closing her eyes as if she were trying to perceive the supernatural energies that reached out to them.

CHAPTER 14
MAELSTROM

David maintained his position in front of the others as Lee Ann got to her feet and began to walk toward the voice. Felicity got up and ran to her side. A loud rumble sounded in the distance, indicating the threat of an oncoming storm.

"What do you see?" Felicity quietly asked her.

Lee Ann looked in the direction of the ruined buildings.

"Nothing yet," she whispered. As soon as the words left her mouth, an orb appeared in the trees above her. Then, at least four other orbs began to appear, dancing like fireflies in summer.

"Wait, they're here," Lee Ann uttered softly as she squeezed Felicity's hand.

Felicity closed her eyes and sensed that the closest entity was quickly making its way toward them. Only Lee Ann could see the orbs as they descended toward the Earth and transformed into the figures she knew but now there were others that she hadn't encountered yet.

Carolyn Gracie's translucent figure was moving toward Lee Ann and her husband was following just behind her. The others were stationed closer to the site where the buildings had once stood. Lee Ann walked toward the site.

"Careful," Felicity urged, grabbing Lee Ann's arm.

"I have to get closer so that I can see the others, so I can see what happened."

"I'm coming with you! Everyone else stay here! Stay close to each other!" Felicity commanded, especially to David who, although obviously shaking, expressed he wanted to come with them.

"Stay here with them, David," Lee Ann echoed Felicity's command.

He reluctantly nodded and stood between the others and Carolyn's figure. David, Jasmine, and Katrina could now feel and hear the presences gathering around them, although they couldn't see them. They were all feeling overwhelmed and frightened as the reality of the spectral presences washed over them. No one said a word.

As Lee Ann drew closer to the ruined site, the distance between her and Carolyn evaporated. They were almost right next to each other.

"Please help us. They are coming! The men from town, they've found us!" she called out.

Lee Ann paid little attention to this, having had this same encounter with Carolyn many times before. She was determined to see what had happened here and who the others were. Lee Ann shone the flashlight out into the night but it appeared that a fog had descended into the hollow, diffusing the beam. As the foundation of the old house came into view, she saw two figures take off into the woods and heard a motherly voice that called after them:

"Quickly, now is your chance! Run children!" The voice was strangely familiar to Lee Ann.

The two figures that Lee Ann spotted running off into the distance were different from the rest. They did not appear as orbs, nor did they appear to be translucent. Instead they were silhouettes, appearing to her senses as living and breathing human beings, but Lee Ann struggled all the while knowing this was impossible.

"There's something different. Two of the figures are different; they moved off toward the east, into the woods," Lee Ann said to Felicity, who closed her eyes to try and perceive what she was saying.

"Yes, they are but the shadows of the living. Not all of them met their end here," Felicity encouraged.

Their conversation was interrupted by the sound of men's voices and the baying of a hound that were approaching from the west.

Lee Ann tried to grab a moment amidst the chaos to wrap her thoughts around what she was witnessing when something miraculous occurred. In place of the cracked stone foundation, the walls of an A-frame cabin arose—it was probably only big enough to contain one or two large rooms. Then, in place of the burned and rotting timbers, a wooden barn with a tin roof clearly formed. Lee Ann saw two more figures emerge from the door of the recently materialized cabin; it was the translucent figure of a fully dressed black man carrying a gun and the timid figure of who Lee Ann assumed was his wife behind him, wearing a nightgown. Seeing her, Lee Ann recalled the figure in her dream—it was the same woman.

The motherly voice that had called out to the children called out again. Lee Ann was close enough now to see that the voice came from behind the large tree that stood in between the cabin and barn at the edge of the woods. It suddenly dawned on Lee Ann that the voice was the same one periodically giving her advice in her head.

"James, you and Wanda have to leave now. Quickly, I'll hold them off. Catch up with the children!" The motherly woman called out.

The man, James, nodded his head, took his wife's hand and ran after the children. As James drew closer to Lee Ann and Felicity, he paused.

"Help us!" he implored them. He seemed both fearful and puzzled as if he had not expected to see them.

"You must realize that your fate has already been decided. You do not have to continue to experience this any longer," Felicity said to him.

Lee Ann watched as the still-translucent figures of the frightened man and his wife looked confusingly at the two of them. This moment of bewilderment was quickly cut short by the sound of a gunshot, which echoed through the forest as if it had bounced off the walls of a canyon. The shot struck James' right shoulder. He fell over backward, just a few feet from where Lee Ann stood. He cried out into the night, his voice echoing until it was swallowed up by the very air around him.

"James, NO!" Wanda cried out and fell to her knees beside her husband.

At that very moment, the sky opened up and the rain began to fall. The thunder sounded again, louder this time.

Lee Ann put her hand up to her mouth to stifle a scream, while Felicity grabbed her other arm and tried to pull her away.

"Lee Ann we must go!" Felicity implored.

"No! We have to help them!" Lee Ann said, taking a step toward the balling woman.

At the edge of the woods, first one cloaked figure, then another emerged from the trees. By this time, the rain was coming down in torrents.

Felicity stepped backward, still pulling Lee Ann to urge her to move away; she perceived negative energies emerging from the woods. Felicity had had some experience with such entities as these before and she didn't want to risk any harm to Lee Ann or the others. She knew that there were documented instances where entities attempted to possess or harm the living.

"There, get her!" A voice cried out indicating Wanda who turned toward the source of this voice. The sight of the man shook her from her sorrow and she broke into a run through the woods following where the children had gone minutes before. She did not make it far before a shot tore through the air right past where Lee Ann was standing and found its mark.

Lee Ann ran instinctively toward Wanda with Felicity right behind her.

"Lee Ann, we have to get your friends and leave here, NOW!" she yelled, but Lee Ann was determined to help the wounded woman. She broke free from Felicity's grip and ran to the figure, feeling an over-whelming sense of helplessness coupled with déjà vu. The blood ran from the wound in the woman's chest down her arm and disappeared into her curly locks as her open eyes stared into the void.

"No, no, NO!" Lee Ann cried out in distress. The menacing, hooded figures made their way toward them.

Felicity put both of her hands on Lee Ann's face and turned it toward her.

"Listen to me, Lee Ann. You cannot do anything for her now! We must get back to the others and get out of here. Trust me! The time is not right for you to help them just yet!"

Lee Ann shook herself out of the trance-like state she was in, nodded, and got to her feet. She quickly followed behind Felicity, who was making her way back toward the campfire. David and the others had already gathered as much of their stuff as they could to hasten their retreat and were huddled in the tent with the screen open so that they could see out. As Lee Ann and Felicity stepped into the firelight, the others gazed at them with astonished expressions from the entrance of the tent. Everyone was damp from the continuing rain.

"Come on, everyone. Let's go!" Felicity called out.

Lee Ann turned back toward the house and barn to see two of the hooded men emerge from the woods carrying torches that the rain would not extinguish. One set fire to the barn while the other went inside the house. The flames leapt out of the windows of the cabin within moments, casting an orange glow about the clearing, undaunted by the storm. Shots flew out from behind the tree as one of the klansmen cried out. He had fallen over backward, dropping the rifle he was carrying. Two more of them began to advance toward the campfire. Other shots rang out but Felicity pulled on Lee Ann's arm again, urging her to leave.

The group ran toward the hill that climbed out of the hollow, leaving the tent behind. The ground beneath their feet became soft and muddy in spots. Felicity quickly led the group while David and Lee Ann brought up the rear. Lee Ann turned around as they crested the hill to see how far away their pursuers were, although she was uncertain as to whether the specters of the klansmen were chasing them or the children that had escaped. Although she couldn't see anything through the ceaseless wall of falling water and moonless dark of the forest, she could hear rustling movements through the underbrush.

"Keep running! Don't stop!" Felicity called out to all of them.

"Come on!" David called to Lee Ann, taking her hand. She turned to flee with the others. The group ran as quickly as they could along the path, Felicity guiding them with her flashlight through the dark night, their clothing now drenched, shoes caked with mud.

Although she could not see them, Jasmine, who was right behind Katrina, could sense the presence of evil entities drawing nearer. She experienced an unsettled feeling of dread just before tripping over a large oak root that stretched across the path. Something unseen grabbed her by the hair and pulled her up to her knees. A sound, like the cocking of a rifle, echoed through the trees.

"NO!" Jasmine cried out.

Lee Ann ran over to her. Beside the trembling figure of Jasmine was a skinny, translucent man who had pulled the hood of his robe back to reveal two beady eyes, glaring with angry malice. He took aim at Jasmine's head.

"Got you now!" he snarled as Lee Ann grabbed Jasmine's arms and pulled her to her feet. Jasmine's flight response had taken over again and she ran blindly into the night, following the others. The man took a shot that went wide and seemed to disappear among the trees.

"Dammit!" he called out from behind them.

"Run!" Felicity called out from somewhere in front of them. Lee Ann followed closely behind Jasmine, not bothering to look back again until they cleared the wildlife refuge. Even here, though, the group did not pause, knowing that the pursuers would not give up the chase at the property boundary. Indeed, the group ran all the way back to where the woods gave way to the Daniels' garden.

Lee Ann pulled at the back door, only to find it had been locked. Trembling, she reached into her pocket to find the keys, knowing that the men that had been chasing them would likely emerge from the wood's edge at any moment. She found the keys, opened the door and ushered the others inside, closing and locking it promptly behind them.

The five of them removed their muddy shoes just inside the door. They moved to the couches in the living room and sat there stunned into silence, struggling to catch their breath and come to grips with what they had just experienced. Shirley and Charles were asleep in their bedroom, and with the dampening sound of the rain they hadn't heard a thing. Lee Ann was the only one who stood up, looking through the windows of the kitchen. A shiver shot up her spine as she saw two hooded figures moving along outside of the house; they seemed to be moving along the energetic boundary that she and Felicity had set up. Soon, they gave up and disappeared.

Lee Ann left and came back a second later with towels for everyone.

"You're safe now," Felicity said to her quietly, perceiving her thoughts.

Lee Ann turned toward the others, grabbed a blanket that had been folded on the seat of a chair and went to sit on the couch beside Jasmine whose eyes were still wide with fear. Placing the blanket over Jasmine's shoulders, she tried her best to smile and offer words of comfort.

"It's okay, they've gone," Lee Ann calmly stated.

"Yes, we are safe now," Felicity concurred as she attempted to comfort Jasmine, who was now crying.

"I am so sorry," Felicity said, shaking her head. "I didn't realize the peril we would face, or I would have never allowed all of you to come. I did not expect those men to interact with us. I thought they would continue to pursue only their victims caught in the endless loop."

"What did you two see out there? I couldn't see anything but I could hear what sounded like a hunt . . . for people!" Katrina's voice trembled with fear.

Slowly, Lee Ann explained to them what she had witnessed. The group sat silently trying to take it all in.

David finally broke the quiet that followed her explanation. "I knew it! I knew something terrible had happened out there and I knew it wasn't a thief's colony. They killed those people in cold blood; hunted them like animals!" He was overwhelmed with fear and anger.

"There is nothing you can do to change what's happened here, David," Felicity patted his shoulder reassuringly.

"But why? What did those people do to deserve such a fate?" Katrina bemoaned.

"Unfortunately, we know very little about that. Obviously, those Klansmen did not like what was happening in the colony. My guess is that it is because there were white families living together with a black family, but my instincts tell me there's more to it than that. Unfortunately, people weren't as open-minded in those days. There were lots of people who discriminated against others simply for the color of their skin. It would not have been uncommon for the Klan to employ scare tactics if there was an interracial community," Felicity said.

"But they didn't just scare them—they killed them!" Katrina shuddered.

"Yes, unfortunately that sort of thing happened in those days, but my intuition tells me there's more to it," Felicity replied.

"Yes, but there's no record of any of this. The newspaper made those men sound like heroes protecting the community from the threat of criminals. We know now that was a lie. They made up the whole story to cover up what actually happened. We still don't even know who they were or why they lived out there. Still, I feel as if there's more to the story as well, but I can't say what," Lee Ann lamented, pacing about the room. The fear that threatened to overwhelm her in the woods had all but vanished, leaving her to ponder the myriad questions in her mind.

"We should tell the authorities. Shouldn't they know what happened out there tonight?" Katrina insisted.

"Tell them what?" David asked, "That we heard the sound of a phantom group being gunned down by phantom klansmen that chased us through the woods? You can bet what Sheriff Donelson would say about that. He would try and send us all to the crazy hospital."

"Unfortunately, David is right. What's important now is finding a way to break the cycle in which these poor souls are trapped. Their traumatic deaths have made them unable to transition. They still need someone to show them the way," Felicity insisted, directing her gaze toward Lee Ann as she said this. Even though Felicity indicated Lee Ann's need for involvement, she didn't force the issue. She was well aware that the time for action had not yet come.

"It's so crazy how these souls don't know they've passed on. They must need someone to make them aware of their fate and open the door for them to cross over. Lee Ann, you have got to help them," Jasmine uncharacteristically implored.

"Why me? Shouldn't Felicity be the one? She's the psychic. I'm just a girl that can apparently see dead people," Lee Ann declared defensively.

Felicity shook her head, looked down at the rug, and then back at Lee Ann who was still pacing about, looking out the windows.

"My girl, you are so much more than that. I can only feel the energies but you can actually see them." Felicity paused, allowing her words to sink in. "There's something else too . . . there's a particular attachment that you have to this place, to the people in it, to the events that took place."

Lee Ann crossed her arms stubbornly, only turning toward Felicity after a long pause.

"I know what you mean but I can't tell exactly what the connection is. There are two peculiar things I noticed out there tonight. For one, two of the people I saw, who I believe were children, were not like the rest; they didn't look like ghosts—you couldn't see through them. It seems that they escaped, that they weren't killed by the men."

"Well, I wonder if one of those children may have been my grandmother. She survived," Jasmine offered.

"Yes, I think I saw her," Lee Ann pointed out, hopefully.

"What was the other thing you noticed?" David asked, leaning in.

"There was a woman hidden behind a tree near the house. She was shooting at the men, trying to protect the others. I think she got at least one of them. Anyway, there was something oddly familiar about her voice."

"Maybe you heard the voice before, she could have been one of the ones that asked you for help," Katrina speculated.

"No, tonight was definitely the first time I'd heard her voice out loud. All of the other times I heard a voice crying out it was Carolyn's voice. I'm guessing that she and her husband gave the klansmen more of a chase than the others, managing to get further away before they were finally killed."

"I suppose that makes sense," Felicity concurred.

"They were also the first figures that I saw tonight; the first ones to leave the cabin."

"Wait, what do you mean it was the first time you heard it out loud?" David asked.

"Well, a female voice has been speaking to me from time to time, telling me I must help those spirits, but in a reassuring way," Lee Ann explained.

"Ah, that's the connection that you have with this place that I've been speaking of. Who do you suppose the voice is? Search your thoughts," Felicity encouraged.

"It's my great-grandmother, Patricia, isn't it?" Lee Ann instinctively replied.

"Yes my dear, it is."

"But why?"

"Because she wants to help you," Felicity reassured her with a kind smile. Lee Ann had questions but she let it go for the time being as exhaustion began to set it.

The events of the evening seemed to cast a silent pall over the group for several moments, each one of them pondering what they had experienced and learned that night. Only the sound of Charles and Shirley coming downstairs broke the silence.

"What's going on? Why are all of you here and not camping in the woods and why is this boy here? I thought we said no boys!" Charles declared, his hair disheveled from having just woken up. He looked a bit ridiculous in his pajamas with his hair standing up on one side. Lee Ann couldn't help but laugh at this. He looked out of the window and noticed the pouring rain.

"Dad, he showed up on his own after I told him he couldn't go," Lee Ann explained.

"Oh, I see," he said softly, seemingly appeased. "Nothing like a good rain to spoil a camping trip." He turned his attention toward his daughter who wore a look of anger and astonishment. "What is it?"

"Dad, I think you better have a seat. What I have to tell you might be hard to swallow standing up," she replied. He looked at her and then over to Shirley who looked just as bewildered as he was.

Both Shirley and Charles sat down on the loveseat, which were the only seats left in the living room, and looked at Lee Ann intently.

"Alright, shoot. Tell us what happened out there," Charles insisted.

Once Lee Ann finished explaining everything, everyone, including her fellow campers, sat stunned and silent. After her story, Charles and

Shirley did the best they could to make sure everyone was comfortable on the couches and in spare bedrooms, but no one was able to get much sleep that night.

CHAPTER 15
YOU'VE GOT NO BUSINESS

W ith the rising sun, Lee Ann got up and walked over to the kitchen to make coffee, lost in her own thoughts.

"Soon you will need to help them," Felicity spoke, startling Lee Ann a bit; she hadn't realize anyone else was awake.

"As long as you are there to show me," Lee Ann said as she loaded the coffee grounds.

"Of course."

"I still don't know what my parents think of all of this. They didn't say much last night," Lee Ann remarked.

"It's a lot to take in. I'm sure their minds are full of questions, as are the others'."

"They aren't the only ones. I have to ask—and don't take this the wrong way—but are you withholding information from me about what I will need to do when the time is right?" Lee Ann's eyes searched Felicity's earnestly.

Felicity smiled and took Lee Ann's hand in her own.

"I am not trying to keep things from you, dear. Trying to explain everything verbally may only confuse the issue. Suffice it to say, the anniversary of all of these events is coming in a few days. My experience has shown that this will likely intensify the events that we've been witnessing out there. It is the perfect opportunity for you to intervene and show them the way."

"Now you're just confusing me more. You still won't tell me how I can show them." Lee Ann's frustration was evident in her voice, which cracked slightly.

"Lee Ann, you are holding onto so much fear and loss. This is what you must let go of for your own sake and in order to free those poor souls. When the time comes, your intuition along with my guidance will be enough to show you how to do that. You will and must conquer your fear at the moment that you feel most overwhelmed by it. Trust me." Felicity's reassuring smile and tight grip eased Lee Ann's frustration and she returned the smile.

"Ok, I trust you," she replied, her heart now filled with a warming reassurance brought on by Felicity's words.

Shirley came down a moment later, still in her nightgown. She smiled politely at Felicity and walked over to the coffee maker to check on its progress.

Lee Ann stood near the back door, looking out into the garden. More thoughts than one person could handle filled her head.

"Quite a night last night. I guess the morning has a calming effect even when you've been through what you all have been through," Shirley said, breaking the silence.

"Yes, I want to thank you for letting me stay here," Felicity responded.

"No problem. You know, I have to say, you aren't what I expected," Shirley admitted.

"Oh?"

"Well, you know people in this town talk, and many of them say not-so-nice things about you. Some say that it's not Christian to believe in the things you do; they also say you're a fake. I guess I expected someone a little less down to earth. You seem very, um, grounded," Shirley shared.

"Ah, that's nice to hear. I'm fully aware of what people think but I've had quite a few years to develop a thick skin."

"So why not go somewhere where people might be more open-minded, you know, like a bigger city?" Shirley asked as she poured her coffee. Felicity laughed to herself, having answered the same question for the children the previous night.

"I have roots in this area and no desire for big cities. I've been to Memphis and Nashville several times. It's alright for occasional visits but that's about it. I have a sister in Franklin, just outside of Nashville."

"Same here . . . born and raised."

"So, I have to ask you: how are you feeling about what took place here last night and what Lee Ann told you?"

Shirley sighed and turned toward Lee Ann, who was now seated at the kitchen table, still lost in her own thoughts.

"Well, I was skeptical when all of this first started, but then I could hear the voices that Lee Ann heard and there was clearly no living person out there in the woods making those sounds. I'd heard about the legend for years but I never questioned it until now. People have been hearing the voices for a long time but no one's ever experienced anything like what Lee Ann has seen and what you all experienced last night. At least, not that I've heard about," Shirley mused.

"So, do you believe everything Lee Ann told you?"

"Let's just say I'm more open to the possibilities than I once was."

"That's much more than most around here can say."

"So, is there any way to end what's going on? I don't think we can stay here if this continues. It's like a curse or something. Lee Ann's been through a lot," she affirmed, turning to her stepdaughter, who was now listening and smiling at her.

"Yes, we are going to help those lost souls find their passage to the next plane. It's always been open to them but they have been too attached to this place and the horribly traumatic experiences they've been through to notice it. They will perpetually live out the horrors of that night if we can't find a way to assist them. We must help them to release themselves and find their way."

"What kind of plane?" Shirley inquired.

"I am only just beginning to understand, myself. I've been given glimpses of it by those that have communicated with me from beyond."

"Well, if you can make it all stop, I'm for whatever hoodoo voodoo works," Shirley said, making Felicity laugh.

One by one, the others woke up. Everyone remained surprisingly quiet about the previous night's events, as if their experience had been some mad, collective dream that faded with the sunlight.

"See you at school," David stated simply to the others as he left. "Lee Ann, I'm here if you need anything," he said as he gave her a hug. David paused to gaze into her eyes, indicating his increasing fondness for her. Lee Ann felt a sudden shyness due to the intensity of his gaze.

"I know, thanks," she answered.

Jasmine and Katrina both hugged Lee Ann.

"Thank you for being here with me," she told them.

Felicity took Lee Ann's hands in her own as she stood in the doorway.

"I'll be back soon. We will complete what we've started. Be brave and strong. Be the way that she would want you to be—you know who I mean," Felicity said, responding to the puzzled look on Lee Ann's face.

The next couple of nights, Charles elected for them to stay at the Winston Hotel on Main Street in town to give them a change of scenery and give Lee Ann a rest from the demands being made on her. They even let her miss two days of school. When Lee Ann got out of the room to walk around town, she swore that people were turning to look at her, although it could easily have been her imagination. It was true that in a town like Laverne, nothing stayed secret for long.

Back at school, Lee Ann also noticed something; it still felt much the same way as when she first came to Pearson County High, like she was a freak on display, the new kid no one was sure about.

Lee Ann immediately found Jasmine and Katrina in the schoolyard talking to each other. They both smiled as she walked up and hugged each of them.

"Hey guys. How are you?" she asked them.

"I've been having nightmares," Jasmine shared.

"I've had trouble getting a full night's sleep," Katrina stated.

"I'm so sorry, you guys. I feel like I've pulled you into something that you'd be better off without."

"Are you kidding? I'm a part of all of this, too. My grandmother was part of it. I want to know everything about what went on out there and help in any way I can," Jasmine insisted. This new conviction to get to the bottom of her great grandmother's fate along with her increased comfort level with her new friends had changed her demeanor.

"Do you think you can ask your grandmother again about her story? Do you think she would tell it to us?" Lee Ann solicited.

"I've been thinking about it nonstop since the other night but I've been trying to get up the nerve to tell her about the, eh, supernatural stuff that happened. I'm going to call her soon," Jasmine answered.

"Great! That could really shed some light on things," Lee Ann pointed out. Just then, her eyes met David's from across the schoolyard. He was talking with his usual friends but the group seemed to be smaller from what Lee Ann previously remembered. All of the four boys in the group stared at her in a way that contrasted with the way they had done so when she was new to the place. Now, their eyes held disbelief, almost disdain.

"Hey guys!" David greeted, in his usual flippant, cheerful manner as he hugged each of them, keeping his arms around Lee Ann a bit longer than the others.

"What's up with your friends? They seem a little transfixed," Katrina commented.

"Why do you always have to use such big words?" he teased. Looking back at them, he saw what Katrina meant.

"I don't know what their problem is," he said, although the tone in his voice belied his honesty.

"What did you tell them?" Lee Ann asked, crossing her arms.

"I didn't tell them nothin', I promise," he insisted.

"So who did you tell?" Katrina pressed, knowing he was holding something back. The three girls stepped toward David as he took a step backward.

"Well, I might have let something slip when I was talking to Sean but he swore he wouldn't tell anyone."

"And you believed him?" Lee Ann asked, all the while shaking her head.

"Sorry guys. Sean is my bud and we tell each other most things."

"Wow, never thought I'd see the day when a guy had more trouble keeping a secret than an entire group of girls," Katrina commented.

"Well, the damage is done now. How much did you tell him?" Lee Ann inquired, not able to hide the annoyance in her voice.

"Eh, well, pretty much everything," he confessed.

"And did he believe you?" Lee Ann interrogated, moving in closer to him.

"He believed the part about the sounds we heard. That wasn't much of a stretch since hunters and such have claimed to hear things for years. He seemed a bit more skeptical about what you experienced."

Just then, Mary, Lisa, and Jenn came up behind David.

"So, you've been off ghost hunting with these losers?" Mary chided. David looked behind him at Lee Ann and then back to Mary. Lee Ann continued to look at him intently, raising her eyebrow slightly in anticipation of what he would say.

"You bet I have. Something happened out there that was wrong and it was covered up. We're just trying to figure out what it was. Get to the bottom of it."

"My dad says you don't know what you're messin' with. He says you had better leave well enough alone," Lisa replied menacingly.

"Whatever happened out there deserves to be brought to everyone's attention. It doesn't matter whose reputation it might destroy and I, for one, intend to do everything I can to find out the details," Lee Ann said pointedly.

Lisa, Jenn, and Mary all looked at each other.

"What actually happened out there?" Jenn asked after a slight pause.

"Jenn, you don't actually believe any of that hooey do you? I mean, they are obviously tryin' to get attention. So pathetic," Mary said, flitting her long eyelashes slightly as she pulled her expensive purse back onto its proper place on her shoulder.

"No, we're not! Listen you guys, I don't know exactly what I heard and felt out there but there were some presences or something that scared the hell out of me, " David announced, his pupils dilated as if someone were shining a bright light in his eyes. Everyone looked at him, captivated by his seriousness.

"Well, I don't believe in ghosts or haunted places, David Franklin. To be quite frank, I'm not sure you do either. I think you might be using this as an excuse to make out with three freak chicks at once," she chided, looking to the other two for backup as she laughed alone. Jenn rolled her eyes slightly. Lisa took a deep breath and looked at the floor, not knowing what to think.

Lee Ann glared, took a step forward and prepared to give Mary a piece of her mind when the school bell rang. This signaled that they only had five minutes until the late bell. It broke everyone's focus, including Lee Ann's.

"Well, gotta go, losers. Let's talk ghosts some more at lunch. It's a date," Mary stated, earning a giggle from Lisa. Mary smiled at her, knowing that at least one of her minions was back on her side.

Lee Ann's rebuttal would have to wait.

"I think you almost broke up the terrible three there," Katrina pointed out.

"If only. At least you made them think, even if it was just for a second." Jasmine's words gave Lee Ann some measure of comfort, making her smile.

Lee Ann was preoccupied with the prospect of going back to that dark hollow, of putting herself back into that infernal loop, seeing those hooded figures just behind her again. She knew from what Felicity had said that she would have to return there and help them somehow. Her confused thoughts were trying to come up with a reasonable way to help these people cross over but she had no idea how to help them, no idea what to look for, or what to direct them to.

Why doesn't Felicity just do it? Why does it have to be me?

"Lee Ann, are you even here today?" Katrina burst into her thoughts. It sounded like a shout, even though Katrina was talking at a normal volume.

"Sorry, guys. Trying to process everything that's happened and trying to figure out what to do next."

"Understandable. Man, ghost hunters would kill to have had the experiences we've had in just the last couple of days," Katrina said. "I'm still processing what happened. It was confusing, all of the noises and just . . . I don't know . . . I can't quite describe it . . . a feeling of foreboding, I guess."

"Leave it to you to be the walking thesaurus. Hey, maybe that can be your nickname. Hey Thesaurus, come over here, I can't think of a word I'm trying to think of," Jasmine joked.

They all laughed at this. Lee Ann smiled, thinking how cool it was that Jasmine had become comfortable enough around them to make a joke.

"So when do we go back out there?" David asked as they rushed through the front door. They only had about two minutes to spare to avoid the late bell.

"Who said anything about we?" Lee Ann answered as she stopped in front of her locker and began to quickly turn the dial.

"Well, we've got to help you. You know, at least be there for you to help protect you," David insisted.

Lee Ann finished turning the knob, looked over at David and smiled.

"Honestly, that's very sweet, David, but there are some things people have to face alone. I can't expect you and the others to risk your own safety for me. Although I wasn't sure, it seemed like we were in real danger. I felt as if those men were going to kill us when they caught up to us, even if they really died long ago."

"I know, I felt that way, too. I was terrified," he admitted.

The bell announced that they were officially late. David shrugged his shoulders and backed away from Lee Ann, making his way to his Spanish class. His eyes flashed a look of longing and frustration, again revealing his growing feelings for her.

"I won't give up askin' to help," he called out. Lee Ann returned his smile, then ran to catch up with Katrina and Jasmine who were already walking into Biology class.

When the last bell of the day rang, announcing the end of classes, Lee Ann practically ran to her locker. She grabbed her Science, English and Math books that she needed for homework and made for the back door. Katrina and Jasmine were stopped at their lockers. As Lee Ann opened the door to leave, Jasmine waved at her. She paused to wave back but kept going through the door. She knew that Jasmine and Katrina would want to go with her to offer whatever support and assistance they could, even if they were afraid; Lee Ann didn't want to drag the two of them into another frightening experience in that dreaded place . . . a place she would have otherwise found beautiful in its rugged setting.

She hurried down her usual route along the pot-holed roads that twisted their way through the forest. A Chevy Tahoe truck pulled up behind her, slowing down. This did not, at first, alarm Lee Ann. Once or twice before people had offered her rides, which she would always decline. Today, she tried to pretend their eyes weren't on her, walking a bit faster along the road but the truck slowed down almost to a stop right beside her.

"Lookie here, boys, it's that witch everyone's talking about," a young man, around twenty with slicked-back, dark hair teased.

Lee Ann cast a glance in his direction and then back at the ground in front of her.

"I don't see any witches around here," she answered with resolve.

"What makes you think there's any reason to go pokin' around out there with Felicity Taylor? Seems like only a witch 'ud be interested in that, am I right, boys?" the driver said to his two friends.

"Yep, you right, Carl. Little lady, you ain't got no business tryin' to dig up stuff that happened seventy somethin' years ago. The dead is dead," an older man said in a deep, gruff voice from the back seat.

"Nobody has anything to fear if they don't have anything to hide," she retorted, looking each one of them in their eyes fearlessly. The driver gradually sped up and the truck went on its way.

Lee Ann laughed to herself, thinking of the disdain she had felt for all of the people of the little town when she first arrived, despite being from here. Now, she had begun to realize that everyone was a product of his or her environment. The reason so many people in Laverne liked hunting and trucks and country living was because it was what they knew and were surrounded by. Being raised a city girl, Lee Ann resisted this lifestyle, but the love for the outdoors was always there, flowing through her blood. She had always found herself out in the woods sketching a holly bush or a cardinal in a cedar tree. One of the things that scared her most was the thought that these experiences with the supernatural would somehow lessen her love of the forest, although deep down she knew they probably wouldn't.

In that instance, she again recalled the funny memory of her and her mother trying to set up their tent in the dark on a trip to Blanchard Springs in Arkansas. When the rain began to beat against the thick canvas walls of the tent, it had buckled inwards and the roof had fallen in on them, the main poles collapsing with it. Lee Ann remembered screaming but then laughing a second later as she and her mother tried to make their way to the entrance.

"Honey, I'm sorry, there's a hotel just down the road. I think it's just too dark out here to do this right now. We'll go stay there tonight," Kim laughed.

Lee Ann smiled at the memory as she reached the gravel drive of her father's house. She used the memory to gather the strength to face her home again.

CHAPTER 16
THE ANNIVERSARY

L ee Ann unlocked the door of the house and walked inside. Surveying her surroundings, she felt as if someone or something might be waiting there. All was silent as the shadows began to lengthen outside in the afternoon sun. Her parents were still at work so she was alone in the house. As soon as she sat down, her phone began to vibrate.

It was a message from David: *Please let me know when you plan to go back out there. Let me help you.*

Lee Ann didn't answer right away but she smiled, thinking of how sweet he was.

A moment later, a text from Felicity came through: *Lee Ann, tonight is the night: the anniversary of the events that took place seventy-four years ago. Things have been intensifying over the past few days leading up to this. This is the night when we will end all of this. I will be there to help you, shortly before nightfall.*

I'll be ready, she texted back, but the reality was that she wasn't ready. She still had no idea what was expected of her and the fear she felt a few nights previously still weighed on her chest, as if someone had actually set a heavy metal object there. The silence of the house, which only seemed to aggravate this sensation, was broken when Shirley entered.

"Well, hi there. How are you?" Shirley asked pleasantly.

Relief washed over Lee Ann and she flashed Shirley a smile that reflected she was glad she was no longer alone.

"I'm better now. To tell the truth, I was feeling a bit nervous being back here after what happened the other night."

"I guess that's to be expected," Shirley conceded as she came over and sat down beside her. "Are you sure you're ready to be back? We can go and spend more time at the hotel if you need to."

"No, thanks. I appreciate the consideration but I have to face this."

"What is it you have to face exactly?" Shirley's face creased with concern as she crossed her arms over her chest.

"I don't fully understand, myself. It doesn't matter, anyway, because tonight is the seventy-fourth anniversary. Felicity says this is the time to try and stop what keeps happening in these woods. She thinks it is our best chance to help those people—the innocents that were involved."

"I don't claim to understand how one can help people that are already gone from this world. I mean, after all, they have already passed."

"I don't either, exactly, but it has to do with freeing them from this never-ending loop of events they keep re-enacting," Lee Ann answered. "Anyway, Felicity is coming over soon to guide me through this and hopefully show me what to do."

"I see. I like her quite a bit. Like I told her, I was expecting someone way different; someone spacey with her head in the clouds, clutching a crystal or something."

Lee Ann laughed at Shirley's preconceived notions of Felicity. She thought for a moment how nice it was to share a laugh with Shirley. She felt at ease around her, something she hadn't felt previously.

Charles came home to find the two of them sitting together talking. The meer site of them brought a smile to his face.

"Dad, I was telling Shirley, tonight is the night that Felicity and

I are going to try and put a stop to this. It's the anniversary of the incident. "

"You have our support," Charles asserted as he slid his arm around his daughter and hugged her.

A knock at the door interrupted their embrace as Felicity, who had appeared only moments after the last sliver of sunlight disappeared, made her presence known. She was dressed for the outdoors, wearing a long black coat, with her multi-colored scarf wrapped around her neck.

"Come in!" Charles encouraged, receiving her warmly.

"How are you?" Felicity cooed, wearing a reassuring smile.

"Alright, I guess. I am sure we'll all be better once this whole curse is gone," Charles added.

"I agree. I am sure it doesn't do much for the property value having a haunted hollow next door," Felicity joked.

"Good to see you again," Shirley interjected, coming over to hug Felicity.

"Likewise." The warmth of their embrace brought cheer to the space.

"So, what can we do to help with whatever's going to happen tonight?" Charles asked, cupping the back of his neck with his hand. He was feeling a bit awkward.

"Just showing your love and support for Lee Ann should suffice," she answered.

Felicity asked Charles and Shirley to stay in the house, although they offered to come with them. The main concern that Felicity had was for everyone's safety, especially after the encounter they'd had last time.

The moon had begun to rise above the hills, lending a silverish light to the tips of the trees. Felicity put her hot cup of tea down on the coffee table and took Lee Ann's hand in her own.

"It's almost time. Shall we?" Felicity stated calmly.

"Ok," Lee Ann agreed, all the while doubting herself as she got to her feet and walked toward the back door.

"Lee Ann, reach down deep. Find that weight that has been sitting on your chest. Search your memories of your mother; seek the love that you feel for her. Let go of fear, the sense of loneliness, loss, and abandonment," Felicity suggested, knowing that as headstrong and righteous as she could be, Lee Ann still struggled with doubt.

Lee Ann nodded, struggling with her belief that all of this was easier said than done.

She reached into a kitchen drawer and pulled out two of the flashlights they had used a few nights before. She handed one to Felicity, and they exited through the back door.. As they made their way through the woods, everything seemed more still and calm than it should have been. The breeze did not stir the leaves as it normally did and the clouds hid the hopeful stars and obscured the moon—making it a dark night indeed.

After taking a deep breath, Lee Ann led the way, crossing the now familiar terrain into the wildlife preserve. Off in the distance, a single owl called out, but none answered it. The lonely quality of the call added to the increasing sense of dread that Lee Ann had been trying to fend off. Nonetheless, she strode onwards with Felicity right behind her.

"So, when are you going to tell me what I need to do," asked Lee Ann when they stopped on the final ridge above the cursed hollow. Felicity was looking at her cell phone to check the time. It was very nearly eight o' clock.

"You will know. Don't worry, I will help you. This is not the sort of thing you can rehearse, unfortunately."

"Why did you say what you did about my mother?"

"You will see," Felicity said, touching her shoulder solemnly, putting an end to the questions.

They began the slow descent down the gradual slope to the floor of the hollow. Everything was still and quiet. Lee Ann focused again on the ruined buildings that were now just ahead of them, only a few short yards away through the trees.

The buildings came into view again, and, along with them, the characters in the scenario took their places in a play that was about to begin its performance, hopefully its final one.

Lee Ann felt fear growing inside her chest, uncertain if it was her own or the characters she saw before her. Her hands began to tingle.

She glanced at them to see if there was any visible sign of what she was feeling.

Carolyn and her husband appeared, just as before; with their pleas, they implored Lee Ann to help them.

"Please!" This time the desperation was more evident in Carolyn's voice. "Please, they are coming!"

"I know," Lee Ann eked out, feeling dread that made her want to shut her eyes against seeing the people meet their rotten fate again. Her chest tightened in anticipation of the arrival of the hooded presences.

Wait, she thought.

This time, something Felicity had said caught her attention and made her think to alter her reaction. This time, Lee Ann took several deep breaths and confronted her own fears. With each deep breath came the realization that the abandonment she'd felt since her mother had gone was somehow tied up with the fear she felt in the present moment. She wasn't afraid of the klansmen themselves, or for her own safety, she was afraid of living without the love of her mother; she was afraid of having to face the loss of her memories again. It perplexed her that these fears occupied her consciousness at that moment. She knew deep down that these fears were somehow related to the super-natural phenomena although she wasn't sure how.

Lee Ann shifted her attention from her thoughts back to the situation at hand. Just as before, the two shadows fled through the back of the house and escaped. James exited the cabin with his gun in hand, and, just as before, he and his wife both collapsed in a hail of gunfire; all the while, the unseen figure behind the tree shot back at the masked men.

Lee Ann was again overcome with the urge to turn and flee but Felicity stood right next to her, took her hand, and held it tight.

"Stand your ground, open yourself up." Felicity nodded, adding, "Let go of your fear and sadness, for they are one in the same. This is what keeps holding you back. It is something that needs to be freed."

Felicity paused to feel her own heartbeat, comparing it to Lee Ann's as it pulsed in her grasp.

"Open your mind! Open your heart!" she called out.

She continued with words of encouragement, urging Lee Ann to release her fears, allow her feelings to open, and remember what her mother's love felt like before it was replaced with this sting of regret, bitterness, and fear.

As the internal pressure inside Lee Ann increased, it created within her a personal storm. She cried out, falling to her knees burdened by the heavy weight she had been carrying. Mentally, she could tell the sensations of this storm were brought about by the emotions of loss she had for her mother. She tried to force herself to let go of her thoughts.

Felicity watched Lee Ann struggle as the energy inside of her gathered more and more force. Her internal storm brewed and from the strength of her soul she began manifesting connections to the energy in the air around her. These connections pulled like strings on the air molecules, which created a wind that whipped at her skin, stinging her tear streaked face and making concentration nearly impossible.

"Lee Ann," Felicity said strongly in her ear. "I know you are afraid. You have the strength to do this. You have more than enough to end this horrible nightmare. Remember, dig deep!" She cradled Lee Ann's hand one last time before releasing it, sending through their touch every ounce of understanding and compassion she could muster.

Feeling this support, Lee Ann again gathered her strength as the energy that was the whipping wind now bent to her will, the part of her that had to save the day. The storm began to clear. On her next inhale, she folded her legs underneath her, instinctively aware of the power this meditative pose would bring her body. For a moment she felt strong, powerful, energized, and then the reality she had been living with hit her again.

No matter what happens here tonight my mother will still be gone. She fell again into the fight, the storm increasing as her fear and loss regained control of her insides. Under this pressure, her mouth dropped open as one of the klansmen stared right at her.

One of the other klansmen turned his attention to the figure behind the tree that continued to fire back at them. The woman appeared, holding her gun and trying to get off another shot. A shot did ring out in the night but it was a shot fired by the klansman.

"NO!" Lee Ann yelled in agony as the woman fell in a heap.

Felicity fell to the ground beside her, taking up her hand again. She held it tight in an attempt to gauge if Lee Ann would crumble under the ever increasing pressure that was growing in her heart. Each minute that passed proved the pressure to be ceaseless.

"Hold tight! Hold tight to the love in your heart!" called Felicity, trying to break into Lee Ann's thoughts. "Go into your heart center. Find the light. Find your love. It's always there. It never leaves. It's the one thing you can always count on."

Felicity pulled Lee Ann's hand to her lips and gave her a blessing, the strength of her entire heritage.

"I insist that the fear leave you! That is all that endangers you. Let it go!" Felicity shouted.

A sudden movement of powerful energy behind them pulled Felicity's attention. It was David, Jasmine and Katrina emerging into the clearing. Lee Ann's friends gathered around them, coming to the rescue.

This support might be exactly what is needed, Felicity thought.

"Listen to Felicity! You can do this. We're here for you!" David shouted as he placed his hand on Lee Ann's shoulder. As each of her friends made physical contact with her, her strength increased and allowed for more clarity of thought. The final contact gave her enough strength to break the hold of the unending fear.

The storm ended as Lee Ann took a deep, cleansing breath. With each consecutive breath, more and more joyful memories of her mother began to dance and shuffle through her mind.

"That's it!" Felicity encouraged as the klansman nearest to them paused. Still, he did not lower his weapon.

Lee Ann held onto the renewed feeling of joy that existed before the memories vanished, leaving her feeling alone and isolated. Looking over at her friends, she felt the love and support their presence provided her.

She squared her shoulders and puffed out her chest. She could feel the fear draining away as the tingling in her hands intensified. Much to her surprise, she felt a great light begin to emanate from inside of her chest and expand outwards and upwards. It lingered in the air above her, then exploded out in all directions, filling the space around them with light. Acting on instinct, she began to realize that in the absence of her fear, she was able to become a conduit for the souls to cross over. The light was pouring through her, using her as the vessel to guide them towards their much needed acceptance of their fate. Free of her fear, her role was becoming clearer. Each step in her journey had helped her move through her grief and realize her abilities, leading up to this final destination. In the moment that her fear and grief subsided, she was open and ready to help the lost entities looking on.

Lee Ann, you must tell them that it is time to move on, to let go of that terrible night. We will guide them together, Patricia spoke, revealing how she was the force working through and with Lee Ann.

"Allow the light to take you. You have suffered long enough. It is time for you to move past this moment in time and let go of what holds you here," Lee Ann stated. In that moment, each of the souls around her heard her words and knew them to be true. They gazed at her in wonder, inspired by what seemed to them to be an unspeakable power.

The light pulsed outwards and before it returned to Lee Ann it moved through each of the souls of the figures in the hollow. As the strength of her light hit the apparitions, it shattered them, beam by beam, and gathered each particle, pulling the klansmen up into the light. The last standing klansmen cocked his rifle but the light gathered up the figure before he could get a shot off.

Lee Ann dared to open her eyes and caught sight of Patricia who had fallen beside the tree moments before. She was now standing up, still sporting the gunshot wound in her chest, but her face held a peaceful smile. Her eyes were kindly and hazel, holding a familiarity that Lee Ann attributed to the most important person in her life: her mother, but she knew the woman was of course her great grandmother.

"It is done, Lee Ann," Patricia said just as the light beam began to scatter her image. Lee Ann rose to her feet and extended a hand toward her just as the light took away the rest of her. New tears streaked Lee Ann's face but in that moment she did not feel sadness.

Intuitively, she knew that the shadow or curse that had been hanging over the area had been lifted. The loop had been broken, but Lee Ann's mind was still filled with more questions. A voice in her mind seemed to be speaking calmly to her.

All will be revealed. You've done wonderfully. I'm so proud of you. Her heart leaped with joy when she realized it was the voice of her mother, Kim.

Felicity and the others ran over to Lee Ann and threw their arms around her, sharing her sense of relief at the disappearance of the apparitions.

Lee Ann pulled away, her eyes moving from person to person, "That woman was my great grandmother, Patricia. Did you hear her? It's done!"

"Your great-grandmother is right, it is done," Felicity softly stated.

Confused, Katrina asked, "What just happened?" She vocalized what David and Jasmine were wondering.

"Let me try and explain what's taken place," Felicity began. "As we discussed once before, some of us have the ability to help others who need to cross over but can't find their way. They are lost because they are holding onto something from their former lives; in this case it was the tragedy of their lives being cut short so violently. Lee Ann is one of those people that have the ability but in order to help them, she first had to let go of her own fear and grief. When she did so, she had removed a block that prevented her from helping these souls cross over to the next plane, an ability that she naturally possessed, but couldn't realize while she was holding onto that fear. She lifted the curse, breaking the loop of events this group of people had been living out for so many years. The light that you saw moving through her and outwards was energy that was gathering them up, transitioning them to the next phase of their existence. This place no longer has its former shadow hanging over it," Felicity stated with her reassuring smile as she looked off into the trees and back to the group. "Let's get you home," she said as she put her hand on Lee Ann's shoulder and stared into her eyes with a kindly, compassionate gaze.

The forest had instantly taken on a new life and was much more vibrant than it had when they had hiked in. In the distance, a group of coyotes began to bay as the moon came out from behind a veil of clouds, lighting the way. In the hollow behind them, a chorus of barred owls began to call back and forth, vying for territory. Now, the forbidden hollow was just another space in between the numerous hills that rose up in seemingly endless succession on the horizon behind the group. Even with all this evidence of change, each of the companions walked back to the house in silence, each lost in their own thoughts and in awe of the events of the evening.

Back inside the house, Charles was pacing impatiently awaiting their return. A couple of times, he went to the door, compelled to go out and help his daughter. Each time, Shirley pulled him back and encouraged him to stay.

"She has to face this without you. It's going to be okay," she said on his last attempt. Charles stared at her for a long moment, nodded his head, sighed and went to sit down. He was greatly relieved when the companions returned unscathed.

"Well?" he said, seeing the look of peaceful resignation on Lee Ann's face.

"It's over," she said.

"But how, what happened?" he asked.

Lee Ann sat down on the couch and took a deep breath. Although she felt great relief, she was completely and utterly exhausted.

Charles sat down beside her, patted her shoulder gently, and was about to ask her more questions when Felicity chimed in.

"Please, let her be for now. We can try and explain later, once she's recovered a bit," Felicity assured him, coming to Lee Ann's rescue.

One by one, the others came over to hug Lee Ann.

"Goodbye, see you at school," David said, kissing her on the cheek. Lee Ann smiled at him and waved to her friends as they left the house.

"I made you some hot chocolate," Shirley came out of the kitchen and sat on the other side of Lee Ann who smiled at this gesture—it was just like something her mother would have done. This time, the recollection filled her heart and made her smile; this time the fleeting memory was not accompanied by a sense of loss or regret.

"I should be going, too," Felicity said as she knelt down in front of Lee Ann.

Lee Ann threw her arms around her neck, feeling hot tears of relief and joy pour from her eyes.

"Thank you for showing me what I needed to do. For showing me what I needed to let go of," Lee Ann said.

"Nonsense. You don't need to thank me. You always possessed the abilities you thought you needed to learn. You just needed me to point you in the right direction is all."

"Please, you will keep in touch won't you? I don't want to lose your friendship."

"There, there, of course I will. You have already learned not to let the fear of loss guide your actions. That fear was the only real threat you faced out there and you have faced it. It will not likely be the last time," Felicity said, holding Lee Ann's face in her hands as they locked eyes before hugging her one last time.

"Goodbye for now, Lee Ann," Felicity said, looking back at her once more before leaving.

Shirley, Lee Ann, and Charles sat in silence for several minutes before Charles got up and turned on the television. The familiar sound comforted Lee Ann and made her laugh. Now, it would seem things could return to some sort of normalcy.

Lee Ann's settling thoughts were interrupted by the sound of her phone vibrating. She pulled it out of her pocket and saw the message from Jasmine.

Hey Lee Ann. Got a call from my grandma. She says she wants to talk to us. She wants us to come and meet with her in person this weekend if you can.

Yes, of course! I would love to. Do you think we should tell her everything that's happened?

We can try. I don't know how much of the ghost stuff she will believe but I think she should know.

Great! See you at school.

"Hey dad, do you think we can drive over to Blue Spruce to talk to Jasmine's grandmother? She was one of the survivors and can probably fill us in on the details," Lee Ann immediately asked for permission, as the idea of filling in all the blanks about the incident filled her with anticipation. Thinking about the prospect of hearing Jasmine's grandmother's story made her temporarily forget her exhaustion.

Charles looked over at Shirley, who nodded in agreement. "Sure, we can do that. Hopefully that will bring even more closure to the situation. The sooner we can close the door on this whole thing, the better."

Lee Ann finally decided to try and explain to her parents what had taken place that night. The two of them nodded periodically, exchanging glances that hinted at skepticism and outright amazement. They elected not to barrage her with questions, noticing that Lee Ann's eyelids were already heavy with fatigue. To them, it was enough knowing that Lee Ann and the beleaguered inhabitants of Thief's Hollow could now find peace.

CHAPTER 17
FULL REVEAL

Lee Ann sat in silent anticipation as she watched the landscapes go by on the trip to Blue Spruce. Jasmine, who sat with her in the backseat, eventually broke the silence.

"I haven't been to see grandma in a couple of months. I hope she isn't mad at me."

"I'm sure she'll be okay. My grandmother used to always say the same thing when I'd visit her. 'Oh, Lee Ann I haven't seen you in so long, my how you've grown. You should come see me more often.' I think she might have her grandma license revoked if she didn't say that," Lee Ann answered as Jasmine laughed.

"You know, I've been wondering about what we should do with all of the information we learn. Do you think we should try and get a story about this whole thing published in the local newspaper, maybe even go to the major news companies and papers?" Jasmine asked.

"I've been wondering the same thing. I do think that people deserve to know what really happened, for sure. We just shouldn't be surprised when most of the people of Laverne try to deny the facts. One thing I know for sure about my home town is that old beliefs die hard."

"That's for sure."

"But yes, I do think we need to get the story out there."

"I know a reporter for the *Laverne Times*," Shirley said upon overhearing them.

"Do you think they'll put out the story?" Charles asked. "Most of her beats are about local bake sales, fishing derbies, and the like."

"Only one way to find out, I guess," she answered. "I think we should reach out to the Nashville and Memphis papers, maybe the news outlets, too."

After about an hour and a half, they saw the sign for Blue Spruce and pulled off onto a winding country road that passed farms and woods until they came to the small town. They pulled onto a short gravel drive with a white shotgun house—a narrow rectangular dwelling with all of the rooms arranged one behind the other. Smoke was rising out of the chimney. There were two cars in the driveway.

"This is it," Jasmine said.

They quickly exited the car and walked up the front steps. Jasmine knocked on the door. Seconds later, her grandmother opened the door, peering at the people through narrow reading glasses. She had her greying hair pulled back in a bun and walked with a cane.

"My pride and joy! Get on in here and bring your friends out of the cold!" she said holding the screen door open. Everyone filed into a sitting room and took turns shaking the woman's hand.

"Sorry I haven't been to see you in a while. Things have been a little, eh, interesting back home in Laverne," Jasmine stammered, feeling a bit ashamed that she hadn't been there to visit in so long a time.

"Everyone, this is my grandmother Roberta Johnson," Jasmine stated. "Grandma, this is Lee Ann, who I told you about, and her parents, Charles and Shirley."

"Very pleased to meet all of you. Welcome to my home. Please everyone find a seat. Oh, how impolite of me . . . everyone, this is my very dear friend, Deidre Gracie." A white-haired caucasian woman who stood behind Roberta nodded to everyone.

"My pleasure," Deidre said.

"So, you're Carolyn Gracie's daughter, then?" Lee Ann asked.

"Why, yes, I am."

"We two are the only survivors of the incident at Thief's Hollow," Roberta said proudly as everyone found their place on the couch opposite the two chairs where the two elderly friends sat down. "We was just reminiscing about the old days."

"Grandma, we've got some, eh, strange news to report. Lee Ann, did you want to tell them the whole story?" Jasmine asked. Lee Ann swallowed hard and could feel sweat forming at her temples. She had no idea how the two survivors would take the details of her story, especially the supernatural elements of it, but nonetheless, she told them everything: the strange calls for help that turned into actual apparitions, the many interactions she'd had with them, the research she tried to do, and the terrible scene of the raid on the colony. During her account, Lee Ann noticed how the two women looked back and forth at one another with expressions that conveyed both astonishment and recognition.

"Well now, that's quite a story, but I have to say I believe every word of it," Roberta finally said.

"Me too," Deidre concurred.

"Even the part about the ghosts and such?" Jasmine asked.

"Child, I have been on this earth eighty-three years and I have seen and heard some things myself. Had the details of your story not matched the facts, we might have cause to doubt you. However, everything that you mentioned did, in fact, take place. Shortly before I called you about meeting with you all, I was overwhelmed by a sensation. It was more like a sense of well-being washing over me. I don't know how or why, but I knew that the curse that was hovering over that hollow had been lifted. I knew something had changed. That's when I knew the time was right to tell you the story. It was just a feeling I had," Roberta confirmed.

"Yes, I, too, felt something, although I find it hard to explain. I've known for years that the place was haunted; the evil deeds of that evening left their mark on the place," Deidre said as she smiled at her old friend.

"So, please, tell us the whole story. Right now all we have are bits and pieces," Lee Ann said.

"Alright, child, I will tell you everything. Let me just say that you look so much like your great-grandmother, Patricia, who we both owe our very lives to. Without her heroism, we probably would have been shot down like the rest of them," Roberta explained. Her gaze became far off as she looked out the window, her mind drifting back to a distant time.

"Thank you," Lee Ann said gratefully.

"So, it all began when my father, James Johnson, began to do some odd jobs for Gerald Langston around 1942. Gerald owned lots of properties, including the First Citizens bank in Laverne. He was well-respected and very well-heeled. My father would walk to the Langston farm and do whatever work was needed. Well, one night, he overheard a terrible fight between Gerald and his wife, Carla, when he was out in the barn cleaning up. He ran inside and saw Gerald push his wife to the ground with all his might. She fell and hit her head and died instantly. According to my father, Gerald and my father just stood there and stared at one another for a moment. My father broke into a run and left the place for good, while Gerald called out for him to stop. Well, my father immediately went home. He and my mother debated about whether or not he should go to the police. He finally decided that he would but just as he was about to do so, a knock was heard at the door. The sheriff had come to arrest my father—Gerald Langston had accused him of murdering his wife!"

The assembled group looked around at one another in awe of this tragic story.

"So, my father and my mother, Wanda, left the house through the back door, escaped into the woods and went into hiding. Not knowing where else to go, they sought out your great-grandfather and grandmother for help, Lee Ann. They, too, would have my father come over and do various tasks for them. After a while, we were as close as family. Boy, I tell you, Patricia Daniels had a heart of gold. She told our family that if we ever needed anything to call on her. They showed up in the dead of night at your great-grandparents' house and told them what happened, saying that they had no one else to turn to. Patricia agreed to help them, but your grandfather, Stewart, did not want to aid a known fugitive. An intense argument followed but in the end Patricia told her husband that she could not stand to see justice being perverted in such a way. She proposed that they journey deep into the woods and live in a remote hunting cabin on their property. He refused to go along with this idea. In the end, Stewart took their child and left, even though Patricia begged him not to. She decided to go ahead with her plan take our family deep into the woods of their family's property. She said that the game was plentiful and that it was remote and hidden enough that they could live there as long as they liked."

"That's where my mother and father came into the picture," Deidre interjected. "You see, my family and yours were very close, Lee Ann. Your great-grandmother and my mother were very good friends. When my mother learned of Patricia's plans, she wanted to join with them— to help the group and live a life of solitude in the forest. In fact, my father had talked for years about how he hated life inside town and wanted to live off the land. So, in the autumn of forty-four, Patricia, my mother and father, and the Johnsons hiked miles into the heart of the forest to hide out from the law and carve out a new life for themselves."

"This was years before the land was sold to the State and later declared a wildlife preserve," Roberta continued. "For many weeks, we lived off of the land, hunting and planting our own vegetable garden. We lived quite peacefully for a short while, although I have to admit I missed many of my school friends. Mother would teach us lessons during the day and then we would fish in the creek or go swimming. We were quite happy, but all of that was not to last. The sheriff and his men finally got wind of where we were hiding out. In those days, there was so much forest, finding someone was like finding a needle in a haystack. To this day we don't know if Patricia's husband told them or maybe they threatened him for information. Either way, they found us. They came in the night and surprised us. It was particularly shocking to see the Ku Klux Klan members. I'm guessing that the sheriff and his men recruited members of the only group that would help them take care of the people that knew the truth about what Gerald Langston did. You see, the sheriff was protecting Gerald from the justice he deserved. All he had to do to get the Klan involved was appeal to their racism and tell them that blacks and whites were living together out in the woods. So, they came for us because they hated us, but mainly because they had to kill everyone who knew that it was Gerald Langston who had killed his wife and not James. Patricia had a plan if we were discovered, but they did catch us unawares. It was about eight o'clock, and I can remember my mother climbing up the ladder to the loft where Roberta and I slept.

"We've gotta get out of here, Deidre!" She whispered. Then, Patricia told us about a landmark deeper in the forest where we could meet up; it was a cave about five miles north of the cabin. The plan was for Roberta and I to escape through the woods and hide out in the cave, once we found it. We were terrified when we heard the sound of the dogs and the men approaching. We ran for the woods as fast as we could, but we could not bring ourselves to leave our parents. We watched the whole scene play out from the cover of the trees."

"When the men burst into camp wearing their sheets, I was terrified. Patricia left the cabin first, followed closely by my father, James. Patricia instructed us to make for the cave and said she would give us cover while we escaped, which she did from behind a tree. The next thing I saw was my father falling over from a gunshot wound. I wanted to cry out to him, but Deidre covered my mouth and held onto me in the cover of the forest. Next, I saw my own mother run from them. They gunned her down like she was nothing," Roberta said as her voice began to crack with emotion.

"I'm so sorry," Shirley said, shaking her head.

Deidre sighed and wiped the tears that began to form in her eyes. "Then, my parents tried to make their escape. They tried to go in the direction that Roberta and I had gone but the men cut them off, making them go east. What I heard next still haunts my dreams, although I didn't see what happened; I could hear the distant cries of my parents being gunned down in cold blood."

"How horrible...," Charles said, sympathetically.

"I am so sorry for your losses," Shirley added.

"What's more, they tried to cover the whole thing up by making up that whole story about the thieves. Everyone believed it and they put an article in the local paper painting the Sheriff and his men as heroes," Roberta said.

"I read that article in the town library. So what happened to the two of you? Where did you go after that?" Lee Ann asked.

"We spent a long night in the cave, listening for the sounds of the dog and the men's voices. We heard them off in the distance but they never found us. Finally, we hiked out of there and came to the small town of Herndon. From there, I contacted my Aunt Gina in Blue Spruce who came and got us and took both of us in as if we were her own children. I have lived here ever since," Deidre reported.

"As have I," Roberta said, smiling at her old friend.

"So did you ever try and tell anyone the real story about what happened out there, Grandma?" Jasmine asked.

"Oh, child, I told anyone who would listen. Anyway, the people I told said I should go to the papers and the news. I was going to but then the threatening phone calls and letters started coming in."

"I received them, too," Deidre confirmed.

"So you were too scared to share your story with the media, then?" Lee Ann asked.

"Yes, at that point we both just wanted to go on with our lives. We knew that Gerald Langston, the Sheriff, and townsfolk who took part in the raid would never be brought to justice. We thought that if I kept quiet they would leave me alone. So, neither one of us ever went back to Laverne and we never went to the papers with our story. Now, most of the people that were involved have likely passed away and everyone believes that the sheriff and his men were heroes on that terrible night. They believe that the community was kept safe from a pack of thieves that were never there," Deidre said, shaking her head.

"How terrible. People need to know the truth. Ms. Johnson and Ms. Gracie, would you two be okay with us taking this story to the papers and news stations? I know you were afraid before, but maybe enough time has passed now," Lee Ann appealed.

Roberta and Deidre looked at each other for a long moment before answering.

"Yes, it's alright with me. The last time any of us received any threats was many decades ago, so I expect the danger has passed," Deidre concluded.

"I agree. As I said when you first came, I knew last night that the curse had been lifted. I knew the time was right for the truth to come out. People can make of it what they will," Roberta said. Everyone sat in stunned silence for several minutes as the details put flesh on the bones of the story they had all played a role in.

"Those men should have been thrown in prison, or worse," Jasmine stated in defiance.

"They will face judgment, child, don't you worry. Every man and woman must stand before God and answer for their deeds at the pearly gates. Amen," Roberta said.

"Amen," Deidre said, as she gently patted Roberta's hand.

Roberta insisted that the group stay for lunch. For the remainder of the visit, they talked, laughed, ate homemade fried chicken and vegetables and put the incident to rest. Only when the group was set to leave did Roberta mention anything about that fateful night again.

"Girls, do not expect anything to change once you've told the story. Folks gonna believe what they believe. I just don't want to see any of you become bitter over this whole thing when you catch some flack over it. You may have people threaten you and curse you, or worse. Just know that for every hateful, prejudiced person there are two or three who will wish you well and even help you if they can. Take people like your Great-grandmother Patricia or Deidre's Aunt Gina, for instance. Without Patricia's help, Deidre and I would have also been haunting those woods. Without Aunt Gina's help, we would have had nowhere to go. I'm just glad to hear that the souls of the deceased can now go on to their well-deserved rest. And you, my dears, can go back to being normal teenagers," Roberta said to them before hugging each one of them.

"Goodbye, grandma! Goodbye, Mrs. Gracie!" Jasmine stated.

"Goodbye, Mrs. Johnson and Mrs. Gracie. Thank you so much for sharing your story with us!" Lee Ann said.

"My pleasure. Come and visit us anytime!" Roberta answered with a warm and reassuring smile.

There wasn't much conversation on the road back to Laverne. Everyone was lost in their own thoughts, in awe of the surviving women and their story.

CHAPTER 18
A TOWN DIVIDED

The next day at school, Jasmine and Lee Ann revealed the details of the story they had heard from Roberta and Deidre to their friends. Neither Katrina nor David could keep their mouths from falling open in amazement.

"Their story matches all of the details of what you saw," David concluded.

"I know, right? I just don't know what to do with the story," Lee Ann added.

"Why? I thought we all agreed that people need to know the truth about what happened out there?" Jasmine indignantly retorted.

"I agree that the truth needs to get out there, one hundred percent, but we have a problem. Another problem besides changing the minds of the people who believe the thief story."

"Evidence, or lack thereof," Jasmine said, realizing the problem.

"What? You mean we aren't going to change the minds of a bunch of people that live in a small town who've heard a certain story for all of their lives? You mean they aren't going to believe us with nothing to back up our story except supernatural encounters?" Katrina interjected.

"Exactly," Lee Ann replied.

"So, you don't think the papers might want to hear the women's story at least?" David wondered.

"I don't know. I don't want to see them experience any more harassment. You know there would be some people around here that would sink that low; people who might not want the truth out there."

"So we're not going to the media with our story?" Jasmine asked, unable to hide the disappointment in her tone.

"I want to but I don't know if it's a good idea, or if anyone would even print the story," Lee Ann lamented, her head hung slightly in resignation.

At the end of the day, the group went their separate ways without discussing the matter further. As Lee Ann began to walk toward the exit, she realized some of the students were giving her strange looks. Some of them were whispering to each other. This irritated her slightly, but above it all, she felt a deep sense of satisfaction and relief. Despite whatever they were whispering about, and despite whatever the locals believed actually happened with regard to the incident, she knew the lost souls who had been involved were now at rest.

In addition, Lee Ann had the blessing of knowing that her grief and fear could be controlled, managed and released. Her memories of her life with her mother were now again moments she would cherish. Like the keepsakes her mother had given her, the memories would no longer be overshadowed by feelings of loss, regret, and abandonment.

As she passed through the schoolyard, she saw David talking to his usual group of friends, many of whom turned to stare at her as she walked past. She saw Mary, Lisa, and Jenn, standing together in a group beside the boys David was talking with. Lee Ann paused for a moment, then proceeded to the road and her walk home. When she reached the end of the parking lot, someone pulled on her arm from behind. It was Jenn, wearing a sympathetic smile instead of her usual haughty expression.

"I want you to know I believe your story. I'm very sorry to hear about what happened to those people out there. I'm also sorry for the way we've treated you. Maybe we can hang out sometime, if that's okay with you," Jenn said.

"Eh . . . um, okay sure," Lee Ann said, completely caught off guard. Jenn smiled before turning to walk back to the group of girls. The rest of them looked at Jenn with a look of disdain, asking her questions that Lee Ann couldn't quite make out. Her eyes were searching the group for David, who seemed to disappear behind some of the boys. She knew that David, as usual, had been unable to keep a secret from his friends. Lee Ann waited for the groups to disperse so that she could get David alone.

"Where do you think you're going?" Lee Ann asked him, crossing her arms as she spied him leaving the parking lot.

"Oh, hey," he greeted, as if he hadn't noticed her standing nearby.

"You told them, didn't you?" She crossed her arms even tighter.

"People deserve to know the truth," he insisted, crossing his own arms in response.

"But I thought we talked about this."

"Yeah, you decided not to take the story to the media. You didn't say we couldn't tell anyone," David insisted. Lee Ann glared at him, knowing that he was right. However, she still wasn't ready to let him off the hook for telling his friends.

"How much did you tell them?"

"Enough."

"What about all of the details?"

"I left out some of the things that might be harder to believe. I just told them about the story the survivors told you and that Felicity had helped you, helped us, to lift the curse on the place."

"You just couldn't help yourself, could you?" She said as she shook her head and turned away from him.

"Lee Ann, wait. I'm sorry! I didn't mean to betray your trust. I just wanted so desperately for people to stop believing that stupid story about the thieves . . . to stop believing that the Sheriff and those men were heroes. They need to know what kind of men they really were. Lee Ann, there are several of us who doubted that whole thief story for years . . . like I said when I first met you and told you about the colony. Lots of people are going to believe you. Trust me."

Lee Ann saw the earnestness in his eyes. She stopped flaring her nostrils, looked at the ground and sighed.

"I know you didn't mean any harm," she acknowledged. "Look, I'll talk to you later. I have a lot of homework to do."

"I will see you soon, right?"

"Sure."

"Hey, Lee Ann, one more thing," he said as she turned around to face him again.

"Yeah?"

"I was wondering if we could go to the movies or something."

"David Franklin, are you asking me out on a date?"

"Maybe," he said.

"Hmm, I'll think about it," she said with a smile that let him know she would likely take him up on the offer.

"Fair enough," he answered as he turned to leave.

After a couple of days, David's account of the incident at Thief's Hollow began to spread throughout town. There were discussions and arguments among people who had lived in the town all of their lives as each person digested the information for themselves. When Lee Ann walked through town, she could feel people's eyes on her. It wasn't long before Shirley and Charles also heard things from the townspeople.

Some of Shirley's friends who always came to their house for bridge night failed to show up.

Some of Charles' mechanics that he'd recently hired to work at his shop also asked him questions. He backed up the truthful aspects of the story they had heard.

"Ken, I wouldn't have believed the story either if I hadn't seen what I saw with my own eyes," he told one of his younger mechanics as they made preparations to open the garage located in the front of their property for business.

"People are talkin'. Some say that your daughter's a witch; that she teamed up with Felicity to lift that curse. Some say she ain't a witch, she just has a gift. Others insist it's a story that they made up for attention. Boy, I ain't heard so many people talk about somethin' since I don't know when," Ken stated.

"So what do you believe?" Charles asked him as he scrubbed the grease off a wrench.

"I don't rightly know. I think anything's possible. I mean, if the sheriff and his boys shot some people in cold blood, it makes sense that they would make up a story to cover it up. I don't see no reason why a couple of old ladies would make up a story like that for attention. If what them ladies say is true . . . it ain't right."

"Couldn't agree more, but the fact of the matter is, none of the people involved are even alive any more, as far as I know. There isn't anyone that can be brought to justice for it," Charles bemoaned.

"A damn shame. Hope those folks rest in peace."

"Yep. Let's get these tools organized. We gotta open this place in less than a week's time," Charles said, bringing his attention back to the task at hand.

Lee Ann decided to go by the drug store on her way home from school to pick up a few things she needed. As she stood in the checkout line, she overheard a conversation between two of the women in the pharmacy.

"Now, Jean, you don't know what you're talking about. There weren't no ghosts in that holler. Them's all just rumors. Same thing with this story about the group that the Sheriff murdered. That's all made up. Everyone knows that there were thieves living out there in them woods, hell bent on robbin' the town. Hell, they murdered someone!"

"No, Laura, that just ain't true. I believe what those women said. What reason they got to lie after all of these years?"

"Why'd they wait so long to come out with their story?"

"Same reason anyone holds onto information like that—fear of people like you not believing 'em. Hell, they were probably worried about their safety considerin' what they knew."

"Hmm, well even if it is true, better to leave well enough alone, I say."

The women stopped their conversation as they looked over at the checkout line and recognized Lee Ann. There was an awkward moment when everyone seemed to be looking at her as she sat her drawing tablet and pens down next to the scanner.

"Will that be all?" the man behind the counter asked.

"That's it," Lee Ann said as she took a breath and smiled. After everything she'd experienced, this scene just seemed funny to her. She realized in that moment that no matter what people believed, it never changed the truth. It had no bearing or effect on the outcome of events. The hollow behind her house was just another patch of wilderness and the souls trapped there were now free, whether anyone believed it or not.

She decided to go by Felicity's place after leaving the drug store to visit her. When Lee Ann started to walk up the steps that led to Felicity's house and place of business, she recognized the unmistakable hobble of Principal Harris as he walked out of the door. His face flushed with surprise and embarrassment when he saw Lee Ann.

"Eh, well good day, Miss Daniels," he stammered, smiling at her from the bottom of the stairs as he turned to quickly leave.

"Hello, Mr. Harris," Lee Ann greeted, trying hard not to laugh. She walked up the stairs and knocked on the door.

"Well, Imogene, you're early," Felicity said as she opened the door. "Oh, it's you Lee Ann. Come in! Come in!" She gave Lee Ann a long hug.

"So, I have to ask what Mr. Harris was doing here?"

"Oh, Jay? He comes in and gets his palm read from time to time."

"He did not like seeing me coming. He doesn't have to worry. I'm not going to tell everyone I saw him here," Lee Ann revealed, making Felicity giggle.

"Sit down," she said.

"How have you been?" Lee Ann asked.

"Fine. Business is booming. Apparently there are more people that believe our story than you think," she shared.

"Yeah, I'm still kind of mad that David told people," Lee Ann recalled.

"I understand, but you mustn't let it bother you. The truth is like the roots of a plant; it always finds a way through the dirt. Now, what people do with the truth when they hear it is a different matter. I just hope that there aren't people threatening you and your family." Just then, Lee Ann noticed that one of the windows facing the side of the house had been broken out. Then, she saw a rock with the word 'witch' written on it that had been placed next to the windowsill.

"I see you've had your own problems," Lee Ann noticed.

"Oh, that doesn't bother me. In fact, it happened once many years ago, before any of this. Perhaps the most important thing to learn from everything is how the true depths of your courage can stop fear from overwhelming you."

Lee Ann smiled and gripped Felicity's hand underneath the table.

"We have had a few threats, letters and phone calls, mostly about what they would do if we took our story to the papers and that sort of thing. However, we have also actually had a few phone calls of encouragement, which surprised me," Lee Ann shared.

"That's good to hear. Part of not giving into fear is accepting the fact that many people are not going to accept you, no matter what you do."

"I know. I feel like I've been learning that lesson my whole life."

"Well, teenage girls are especially bad. I should know. My oldest daughter, Holly was a lot like you."

"I haven't heard much about your family."

"They keep mostly to themselves. The whole psychic thing doesn't have everyone's approval, as you might suspect. I have two daughters, Holly, who lives in Georgia, and Susan, who is a television reporter in Chicago, and a younger son named Ken who lives in Nashville and is a minister."

"A minister?"

"Yep."

"So, I'm going to go out on a limb here and guess that he's the one that doesn't approve of the whole psychic thing."

"Bingo."

"I still have so many questions . . . about everything. Like what exactly happened out there on the anniversary of the incident. Why am I one of the people that has these abilities to see what others can't?"

"I'm not sure I have all of the answers that you need but I will tell you that it is best to be patient and let these things reveal themselves to you, for they will in time."

Lee Ann was a bit disappointed in this answer, wishing that Felicity had given her more of an explanation, but for the time being it was enough to see her again and know that she was doing well.

Felicity sensed this and decided now was the time to reveal something to Lee Ann that she had kept to herself. "Lee Ann, I want to tell you something that isn't a full explanation but it should provide you with some measure of comfort. After I met you, I was contacted by someone that is dear to you; your mother. She sent me a message while I was meditating," Lee Ann's eyes lit up with anticipation upon hearing this.

"What did she tell you?" she anxiously questioned.

"The first time, she told me to help you release your fear. I wasn't sure what she meant, but as I got to know you I realized what it was. Then, just before we camped out at the hollow, she contacted me again to let me know that I had to help you on the eve of the anniversary of the tragedy at Thief's Hollow. I had questions, just as you do, but she would not reveal anything else other than the fact that she was going to reveal more to you when the time was right. I knew then that I needed to help you at all costs," Felicity shared as her face lit up with her comforting smile.

"But, when?" Lee Ann insisted.

"Be patient, my dear. As I've been telling you, all will be revealed in time," Felicity answered as she gently patted Lee Ann's shoulder.

EPILOGUE

After walking home from school, as she did every afternoon, Lee Ann stopped at the end of the gravel drive, remembering how she felt upon first seeing it: she had been reluctant to be here in the middle of nowhere among people with a small-town mindset, resistant towards leaving her old life behind. What stood in stark contrast to the present, more than all else, was the absence of the weight that had pressed against her shoulders and her heart back then; it had impeded her every breath. Now, with the weight lifted, she could see the setting as it was: a gorgeous, though modest, homestead nestled deep in forested hills. Maybe it was because the sun and its shafts of light illuminated pockets of the forest as if celestial beings were holding court in tiny clearings. Maybe it was the fact that it was Friday, which always brought with it its own liberation of time. Maybe it was the oncoming spring, the warming of March and the onset of longer days. Lee Ann knew it was all of these things, but mainly the reason the weight was gone was because she could no longer find a reason to be fearful. The town itself seemed different, more warm and open. She could sense the changes in the faces of the people she passed and the conversations she overheard. The town was coming to grips with its past and the truth was now evident for all who were willing to receive it.

Instead of entering the house as she usually did when she first came home, she opted instead to walk around the back, remembering how she had felt when she first looked upon the landscape, before the voices and visions began. She put her backpack down and got out her sketchbook as she reached the edge of the woods. Thumbing through the most recent pictures, it was easy to see the shadow that had so recently resided over her. She looked at a sketch where she had done her best to depict the scene in the hollow. The sketch showed the burning house and hooded men in pursuit of the survivors, along with the mysterious figure of her great-grandmother peering from behind the tree, poised to shoot. The picture before that one depicted the forlorn visage of Carolyn Gracie reaching out to her from the edge of the woods with a trail of translucent, cerulean orbs scattered at various distances behind her. Indeed, these scenes seemed as if they were from a far off nightmare, or perhaps another lifetime entirely. The innocuous wind bending the tree branches seemed to dismiss the notion that this forest ever held any dark secret. It seemed to deny that it had ever carried Carolyn Gracie's pleas for help through the treetops. Lee Ann turned the page and got out a newly sharpened pencil, doing her best to faithfully reproduce the sun-dappled scene laid out in front of her. Only the sound of her father allowing the screen door on the back of the house to slam shut broke her concentration.

Charles walked down the steps and slowly approached his daughter. It made him smile to see her doing what she enjoyed most, as she had that first afternoon. Only now, she returned his smile rather than resisting his efforts to foster a bond between them.

"Whatcha sketchin'?" he asked as he made his way to the grassy area just outside the woods where she was sitting cross-legged.

"The usual," she said, holding it up for him to see.

"Very nice. You know, I can tell that your technique is comin' along. You seem to pay more attention to detail. Not that I know anything about drawin' and such," he admitted. She smiled back and looked at it.

"I can't tell but thanks anyway."

"You doin' alright, hon? I mean, that was quite a lot you just went through. Most folks would probably need therapy after all that."

"Yeah, I'm doing great, actually. Just still have so many questions about what happened. I still don't quite know how I was able to make all of it stop, or why it was all happening in the first place."

"Well, I reckon there's probably a lot of places in the world that are stained by the bad things that happened there. I suppose it leaves a mark on the place that takes the right person to rub out. Maybe it's just one of those things you don't need to know everything about. Maybe it's enough that it's over."

"That's what Felicity said, but I want to know the reasons why. I want to know more about the abilities and gifts I might have, so that I can use them to some good end."

"You remind me more and more of your mother every day. Her whole life she spent trying to help those around her. If only I had appreciated it more when we were all together," he said as his eyes glanced at something far off in the distance.

"You don't need to be sorry anymore, Dad." Lee Ann grasped his hand. The gesture caught him off guard as he looked back down at her.

"I have a lot to answer for, darlin'. I know it's all behind us now and happened a long time ago, but I don't know if I can forgive myself for breaking up our family." Despite his efforts to restrain his emotions, Charles could feel the slight tremble in his breath and the tears building in his eyes.

"I forgive you. I'm certain that Mom forgives you as well. The last thing she would want is for you to spend the rest of your life living with regret. You have to try and let go of those feelings," she said, clutching his hand tightly in her own. He lowered himself to the ground to sit beside her, throwing his arms around her. They hugged for a long time and sat in silence.

"Thank you." He took a deep breath as he got to his feet.

"Are you sure you're only sixteen?" he added.

"I guess no one would know that better than my father," she replied with a hint of sarcasm in her voice.

"Because you have the wisdom of someone much older," he added.

Lee Ann went upstairs to finish her homework, feeling that she could actually focus on everyday tasks for the first time in a long while. Later, she went out to the front porch swing to enjoy the cool, perfect evening as she put on her ear buds. The sounds of the band Beach House filled her ears. Lee Ann's mind went back to a similar evening many months ago at her old home. Eventually, she closed her eyes and her playlist came to its end. Thinking that she'd fallen asleep, the silence awakened her.

In place of her house, the wooded landscape and the winding gravel drive leading to the road was the blackness of space, punctuated by stars that surrounded her on all sides at varying distances. She gasped for a moment as she looked below her and realized that the porch and very ground beneath her had vanished. Again she was suspended in the night sky amongst the stars. The familiarity of the scene returned to her just as she felt the presence of her mother beside her.

"Mother?"

"Yes dear."

"I have so many things to ask you, so much news to share with you."

"Oh? Would this be about the legend and your great-grandmother?" she inquired, giving her daughter a knowing smile as she took her hand in hers.

"Yes. You mean you already know?"

"I do indeed. Let me just say how proud I am of you for showing such courage. There really was a moment there when you were in real danger, but you were willing to face it for the sake of others."

"I only did what I thought you would have done."

"You did what you needed to do, and your grandmother and great-grandmother are also proud of you. The strength that you found was in you all along, although you had some help."

"Yes, without Felicity I feel as if I might have broken apart out there."

"Felicity, yes, to her I am forever grateful, but there are others that have played a role."

Lee Ann was puzzled by this. Who did she mean, her friends? Her father and stepmother? As if she read these thoughts, Kim continued.

"Patricia has also played a role. You see, she helped set all of this in motion so that you could let go of the fear and the feeling of abandonment that was weighing on you. It was her way of freeing you and breaking the loop of events that took place so many years ago," Kim explained. Lee Ann frowned up in confusion thinking back to the times when an inner voice was speaking to her.

"She would communicate with me and encourage me, but I thought I was setting them free by breaking the curse," Lee Ann argued.

"You did exactly that. All of the others besides Patricia had been stuck in the loop for years and years because they were holding onto life, unaware that they had passed on. Only Patricia was able to move on after the initial event, such was her resolve. Patricia was able to free the others, but she was only able to do so through you, once you let go of your fear and sense of loss. You see, you showed the way forward once your fear was conquered. You broke the loop and freed the others, not just the lost souls, but the whole town as well. "

"Hmm . . . what you told me helps explain how Carolyn acted. When I told her she had passed on, she had no idea. I can also feel a shift in the townspeople. Mom, I am so confused. I feel as if my head is going to explode because of all of the unanswered questions I have," Lee Ann revealed.

"You know all that you need to know for now and more will be revealed in time." She had heard that before.

"Will I see you again?" Lee Ann asked as she turned to take in her loving mother's kindly face.

"I will always be with you," she answered and her voice trailed off, carried away by the air around them. Lee Ann's eyes opened to the moonlit silhouette of tree branches that yearned for the sky. What she had perceived as her mother's voice became one with the breeze that stirred the leaves into a whirlwind on the porch beside her. They swirled and then sat motionless as the wind withdrew, leaving them scattered on the driveway.

The End

ACKNOWLEDGMENTS

I would like to thank Christine Contini for her guidance and assistance in the creation of this book. I would also like to give special thanks to Laura Cantu, Laura Jones, Jeffrey Naylor, Aubrie Nixon, and everyone at Winterwolf Press for their assistance and feedback. I would also like to thank my lovely partner, Raven and my family and friends for all their love and support.

ABOUT THE AUTHOR

Author Russ Thompson has a uniquely southern gothic style. Being born and raised in Memphis, TN, Thompson is well versed in the southern culture that he brings to life in his writing. During his college years, he cultivated a love for writers such as Kurt Vonnegut, William Faulkner, Shirley Jackson, Herman Hesse, Stephen King, and Neil Gaiman and went on to teach Science for fourteen years. In 2014, he published a collection of short stories, *Tales from the Rim*. It established Thompson's voice as a southern gothic storyteller. Many of the stories were based on real Tennessee ghost stories in which Thompson takes the framework of a myth and fills in the details with masterful fiction. Shortly thereafter, he began to write articles for Click Magazine and became a beta reader for Winterwolf Press.

In the spring of 2018, Thompson finished his first novel, *The Loop Breaker: A Beacon and the Darkness*. This story combines southern settings/elements with the struggles of a young person overcoming the loss of a loved one. After the death of her mother, teenager Lee Ann Daniels must leave the suburbs to live with her dad in the country. There she discovers lost souls seeking help from her. As she struggles to uncover their fate, she realizes she can communicate with them. With the help of Fortune Teller, Felicity she manages to free the souls from the loops that have trapped them, at the same time discovering how to release her grief and fear. Russ Thompson was signed as an author with Winterwolf Press and will soon publish his debut novel. After finishing a second collection of southern gothic short stories, he will begin work on his second novel.

Follow Russ on social media:
Facebook: facebook.com/russtauthor
Instagram: https://www.instagram.com/russthompson54/

 facebook.com/russtauthor
 instagram.com/russthompson54

Made in the USA
Columbia, SC
20 October 2020